PRACTICALLY SEVENTEEN

Practically

Seventeen

BY

ROSAMOND DuJARDIN

J. B. Lippincott Company
Philadelphia and New York

Library of Congress Catalog Card Number 49-10520

To Jackie, Judy and Vic

PRACTICALLY SEVENTEEN

Chapter One

PRESENTING THE HEYDONS

*M*y name is Tobey Heydon and I am practically seventeen years old, since my sixteenth birthday was five whole months ago. Actually Tobey is my middle name and my first is Henrietta. My mother got sort of desperate when her third child turned out to be another girl, so she named me for my father. But, thank Heaven, my grandmother's maiden name was Tobey. Otherwise it would have been too ghastly. People might have called me Henny for short and I would have simply died.

Ours is quite a large family, as families go nowadays. First there are my mother and father, who are pretty old, both in their forties. Still they are fairly modern in their ideas. My father is tall and thinnish and has a pleasant face with lots of laugh wrinkles. He claims that any man, completely surrounded by females in his own home, would go crazy without a sense of humor and that he has had to develop his in self defense. Sometimes his wit is a little corny, as is often the case with older people. But none of us mind. He is really sweet, as fathers go. My mother is very well satisfied with him, too. Her only complaint is that his job as a salesman of plumbing supplies takes him away from home on occasional out-of-town trips, during which time she seems to miss him very much indeed.

My mother thinks she is overweight and she is always talking about dieting and losing ten pounds, although compared with the mothers of some of my friends she has a very nice figure. Once in a while, usually when she is thinking of getting a new suit, she does go on a diet for a day or so. But I never knew her to lose more than a few pounds in this way and my father usually succeeds in kidding her out of the whole idea inside of a week. So then she goes back to baking chocolate cake and lemon cream pie instead of giving us fruit for dessert, and everybody's happy. Both she and my father are beginning to get a little gray around the edges, but, as Dad says philosophically, gray hair is the penalty of having a family like ours. And even I will have to admit that things are seldom calm and quiet around our house, or at least not for more than a few minutes at a time. So there may be something in what he says.

My oldest sister, Janet, is twenty-three. She has dark red hair and very blue eyes and the kind of figure that rates admiring whistles on street corners, although she is married to Jimmy Clark, a construction engineer. Also she is the mother of Toots, a bundle of fiendish energy aged three, whose real name is James Kennicott Clark, although no one has had the heart to tell him so yet.

Next comes my sister Alicia, who is twenty and beautiful, if you care for blondes. She is the ethereal type and her eyes are as blue as Janet's and her hair is palest ash-blond and she is always giving it lemon rinses to keep it that way. I don't suppose you can blame her, since it does enhance her fair skin and the sort of angelic look she cultivates. Although she isn't really angelic. On the contrary, Alicia can be very difficult, and who should know better than I, who have had to put up with her all my life? She has just recently got engaged to Adam Wentworth, who is studying to be a doctor and is the son of Mr. Wentworth, who owns the largest department store in town and is quite wealthy, if a teensy bit eccentric. One of Alicia's worst troubles is, she hasn't a smidgin of a sense of humor, although how this can be true of one of my father's daughters is difficult to see. But Adam doesn't seem to mind, so I guess when you fall in love a sense of humor isn't one of the important factors.

I come next and I am older than my sixteen years in lots of ways, I think. I am not so blond as Alicia, nor so red-headed as Janet, but halfway in between. My eyes are brown like my mother's, and go well with my coppery hair. There are a few freckles on my nose, but they are not noticeable at all when I use pancake make-up. Besides, look at all the movie stars with freckles.

Also, I have quite a young sister named Marjorie, but invariably called Midge. She has lots more freckles than I, sandy hair that she wears braided in pigtails, and skinny legs. She may improve, though, as she gets older. Right now she is only eight and my father frequently refers to her as The After-thought, this being an example of one of his more corny jokes.

We live in an average-sized town called Edgewood. Our house is big and comfortable, although we could do with more bathrooms. Two baths and a powder-room, divided among a family the size of ours and predominantly female, does not equal peace and harmony. My mother says, if we girls would only co-operate, it wouldn't be so bad. But Dad blames it entirely on the man who first invented bubble bath. He was a traitor to his sex, my father says, because there used to be a limit to the amount of time a woman could dawdle away in a bathtub, now there is none.

Anyway, our house is quite adequate otherwise and we have a big yard with lots of trees and bushes. In the summer the breeze smells good coming through the windows, what with lilac and flowering currant and mock orange all around. I wish it were summer right now, not only on account of the fragrance, but because in the summer we can sort of overflow onto the porch and the sleeping porch upstairs and it makes the house seem even more roomy.

The truth is, all this winter we've been a little bit

crowded, due to the fact that Janet and Toots have been staying with us. One trouble with marrying a construction engineer is that he is always being sent to the oddest places. And, with a child as young as Toots, you have to think about the climate and the water and milk supply. So when Janet's husband Jimmy had to go to a remote section of Central America a few months back, Mom and Dad insisted that Janet and Toots come home and stay with us.

I wasn't at all averse to the idea. I thought it would be fun to have Janet home again, after four years. But I hadn't taken into consideration how marriage changes a person—and not always for the better. Janet used to be a lot of fun, gay and full of screwy ideas. She was still like that when she and Toots first arrived. But before long she began to get all morose over being separated from Jimmy so long. And lately all she does is mope around and write long letters to her husband, pouring out her loneliness for him, I suppose. And when she isn't writing him, she is worrying about him. It is all very trying and I cannot for the life of me see why she worries over Jimmy, who is a large rugged type, obviously well equipped to take care of himself. But it does no good to tell Janet that.

A few weeks ago she saw a movie called *Tropic Love*, which was all about a beautiful brunette native girl and the disintegrating influence she and the tropics had on an American engineer who was building a dam in her country. She died in the end and it was all very sad and beautiful, but Janet has been worse than ever since then. She threatens to leave Toots with us and go down and join Jimmy and see what is actually happening, although his letters always sound as though he hasn't disintegrated in the least and is still crazy about Janet. All of us, however, have tried to dissuade her from taking such a drastic step. If you knew Toots, you wouldn't blame us. We all love him to death, but he takes considerable coping with. And Dad, particularly, feels that Janet, who is young and resilient, is the one to do the coping, rather than Mom, on whose hands the main care of Toots would otherwise fall. Besides, Jimmy isn't sure how long he'll have to stay in Central America and he is pulling strings like crazy to get sent back to the States. So all in all, it seems much wiser for Janet and Toots to just sit tight where they are.

Another thing that made our house seem filled to overflowing the last few days was the fact that Adam Wentworth was home from college for the Christmas holidays. And while he wasn't actually living with us, he spent a lot of time at our house. One never knew, in going about home on one's own business, when one would come upon him and Alicia. And they are always kissing. Now I, personally, have nothing against this form of amusement, particularly for engaged couples. Still I should think they might want to do something else for a change now and then.

Having Janet at home and Adam around all the time certainly doesn't make life any easier for me. It is very difficult to maintain any glamour whatever in a family with so many women around, especially sisters, who are

8

likely to say anything. One night shortly before Christmas, when I used a picture in a movie magazine as a model and very conservatively applied a little bit of make-up, you should have heard what happened! When I came downstairs where Brose Gilman was waiting to take me to the movies, Midge began to hoot in a very raucous tone. Alicia tore her attention away from Adam long enough to throw a glance of mingled amusement and horror toward me. And Janet said right in front of Brose and everybody, "Mother, look at Tobey! She's got lipstick all the way down to her chin." She frowned then and stared at me more closely. "And isn't that a darker shade than you usually wear?"

"If it is," I said haughtily, "it's because that pale pink stuff Mom approves of is perfectly babyish!"

Dad spoke mildly. "You did go a little heavy on it, honey."

Mom nodded. "Yes, you did, dear. And do stop slumping. You'll have curvature of the spine."

I straightened a little, feeling embarrassment seep through me. Brose hadn't said a word, he hadn't had a chance.

Janet was still staring at me suspiciously. She said, "Tobey Heydon, that looks like *my* lipstick. And if it is—" She got right up and started upstairs toward her room to see.

My heart began to pound.

Mom said, "You'll have to wipe some off, dear. It looks dreadful."

9

Midge demanded, "What you acting so scared for, Tobey? Is it Janet's lipstick?"

I looked at Brose who had been standing by the couch, taking in the whole humiliating scene. His eyes were very understanding and he raised his eyebrows in a questioning way, indicating that I had only to speak and he'd do whatever I wanted.

I told Mom hastily, "Okay, I'll wipe some off," and I scrubbed at my mouth with my handkerchief. There was no time to lose. Upstairs I could hear Janet rummaging in her dresser drawer. "C'mon, Brose. We want to make the first show, don't we?"

He didn't hesitate a second. "Sure we do."

Calling goodbyes over our shoulders we exited hurriedly. In the hall Brose shrugged into his coat and helped me with mine and I grabbed up my bunny fur mittens and earmuffs. Just as the front door slammed behind us I heard Janet call my name from upstairs, but naturally we didn't wait.

Brose is really wonderful. I wouldn't admit this publicly, because it doesn't pay to let your true opinion of a man get around. Either it goes to his head, or some of your girl friends decide to try to take him away from you if he's that terrific. But I am pretty crazy about Brose. He is quite tall and he has brown hair with a little curl in it which he is always trying to discourage by the most drastic methods. Moreover, he is strong and silent, like most of my favorite movie actors. He has great insight, too, and had taken in at once the whole situation we were leaving behind us.

So we ran down the front steps fast, hand in hand. Luckily Brose had persuaded his father to let him use the car, so we hopped in and he drove away quickly. It was quite thrilling, just like one of those hairbreadth chases in a spy movie. Only, of course, my sister didn't actually chase us any farther than the front door.

When we were safe around the corner, I had Brose stop the car under the first street light so I could fix my mouth again with Janet's lipstick.

Chapter Two

THE TRUTH ABOUT SANTA CLAUS

Brose said softly, "Don't let 'em get you down, Tobey. I think you look wonderful."

"Do you, Brose?" I smiled at him.

"Sure. You always look swell, Tobey. I think maybe that's what's eating your sister."

"What do you mean?"

"Well, maybe she's jealous because you look so much prettier than she does with her lipstick on."

"Oh, Brose!" I felt all nice and warm inside. "You're just saying that. Janet's much better looking than I am."

"Oh, no, she isn't," Brose said firmly. "And she isn't getting any younger, either."

"She's almost twenty-four," I agreed. "Maybe that is why she's such a droop lately—she sees life sort of passing her by and her husband's far away and she's growing older and older and what does the future hold for her?"

"Exactly," Brose nodded. "You've hit the nail right on the head."

"Otherwise," I went on, "there'd be no reason for her to be so unreasonable and mean over a mere lipstick."

"Of course not."

Having settled that, Brose reached over and squeezed my hand and I was glad I hadn't put on my bunny fur mittens yet because the touch of his fingers against mine was warm and tingly and made me feel good. After a moment Brose let my hand go and started the car again. We drove on in silence.

I sometimes think the reason Brose is so sympathetic and understanding is because he, too, has suffered. His name is Ambrose, really, but everyone except his mother calls him merely Brose and he has done it all himself! Ever since he was a child he has been administering black eyes and bloody noses, although in many cases intimidation was all that was necessary. But anyway, those things leave their mark on a man's inner nature and while he is bigger for them, the suffering has made him kind and tolerant, too.

The movie we saw was wonderful and so sad. I adore sad pictures but Brose doesn't. However, there was a Donald Duck, too, so we both enjoyed ourselves.

Afterwards we stopped in at Joe's Grill for a barbecue. Joe's barbecues are simply out of this world and he serves yummy chocolate malteds to go with them. Brose had just got his allowance, so the sky was the limit. We each had a barbecue and a malted. Sometimes when Brose is in straitened financial circumstances, we just order one malted and use two straws. But I don't mind. I am not at all the mercenary type and have never liked a man according to how much he could do for me in the way of entertainment.

Besides wonderful food, Joe's Grill has a juke box with the newest records in town, so naturally there is always a mob of people we know there. It's lots of fun dancing in the little open space around the juke box and the men cut in just as they do at the regular dances and it is all very gay and informal. After Brose and I had been there a little while I noticed Adam and Alicia dancing 'way over in the corner, but they didn't see us, at least I didn't think so. Maybe they just pretended not to so Adam wouldn't have to dance with me, although as far as I, personally, am concerned, he is doing me a favor not to, because I think most older men are terrible dancers. And Adam is certainly no exception. Alicia kept her eyes shut all the time because it is a standing rule in Edgewood that when a girl is dancing with her eyes shut she is perfectly contented and doesn't want to be cut in on. Now I am very fond of Brose and love to dance with him, but I make it a point never to keep my eyes shut more than five minutes, because I think it is bad form. And anyway, life is too short.

They left before we did and I guess Alicia can see with her eyes shut, because when Brose and I got home Janet came out of the library with a pen in her hand (she had obviously been writing to Jimmy) and fire in her eye.

She said, "It was my lipstick! Alicia saw you running around with your mouth all over your face. Give it to me this minute!"

I gave it to her silently and Brose squeezed my elbow in admiration for such patient forbearance and Janet went back into the library with her darned old lipstick. It was still quite early, not yet ten, so Brose and I thought we would find some private spot and talk awhile. Although hoping to find a private spot in our home is really nothing more than wishful thinking.

Since Janet was using the library, we looked into the living-room. The fireplace was very inviting with its blazing logs and cheerfully crackling flames, but Alicia and Adam were sitting on a loveseat which was pulled up to face the hearth. Although we had scarcely made a sound, Alicia said, without taking her eyes from Adam, "Go away, you two. We got here first."

Next we tried the dining-room, but Mom and Dad were wrapping gifts in there. The dining table was stacked with intriguing boxes and there was a drift of holly paper and silver ribbon everywhere. Mom seemed to be doing all the work except licking Christmas seals, which was Dad's department. Mom can't bear the flavor of Christmas seal stickum. Every now and then Dad would hold his finger on a contrary knot until Mom got it tied properly. Otherwise he seemed to be perusing a magazine which he had propped up on the table at a rakish angle.

When Mom happened to glance up and see us hovering

in the doorway she gasped and hastily pulled some paper over as many of the boxes as she could cover up. "Oh, Brose—Tobey! You mustn't come in here. Henry—that one! Cover it up."

"We weren't peeking, honestly," I told her.

Dad, who had put his magazine on top of a box that just might contain the taffeta housecoat I'd been hinting for, exclaimed jovially, "You'd better not peek! Santa Claus won't come."

Brose laughed dutifully. "You mean Tobey still believes in him, Mr. Heydon?"

"All my daughters do—my wife, too, for that matter. They must, judging by the things they want for Christmas. They know darn well I can't afford them."

"Go on away," Mom told us. "I simply have to get these things wrapped tonight. In the daytime, with Toots and Midge around, it's just impossible."

"Okay," I said. "We're going. C'mon, Brose."

"Such a house," I sighed, as we went back into the hall.

"It is kind of full of people."

We went on out to the breakfast nook and by some strange circumstance there was nobody there. So I got out the remainder of the devil's food cake we'd had for dinner and a glass of milk apiece and half a jar of ripe olives.

We sat down and Brose leaned across the table toward me with his eyes very intense and said, "Tobey, will you tell me the truth about something?"

"Why, of course, Brose."

My heart felt a little jumpy with excitement, because you have to admit that is a sort of intriguing question for a man to ask. And Brose was so serious.

He went on, still staring at me in that searching way that would brook no subterfuge, "Are you going to like *Ramona* bound in leather for Christmas?"

I guess my face sort of fell because he continued at once in a very disgusted tone, "I knew it! But you can't argue with my mother. She doesn't seem to realize that times have changed since she was a girl."

I said politely, but I'm afraid not very enthusiastically, "Why, anything you care to give me would be lovely, Brose."

I didn't fool him for a minute. "It would not! Besides, it isn't even what I want to give you. But my mother thinks a book is the very nicest thing for a fella to give a girl— especially one of the classics."

I could just hear his mother saying that. I giggled. "If it wasn't one of the classics, it wouldn't be so bad."

Brose laughed, too, and reached out to help himself to several more olives. Then he sobered. "She's already bought it for me to give you. But you look around carefully in the package," he confided darkly, "and you'll find something else. Something I picked out personally. I still got some of my Christmas money left and now that I know how you feel about *Ramona*—"

He broke off at the sound of footsteps approaching. Alicia and Adam wandered into the kitchen, their arms around each other's waists.

Alicia widened her eyes at sight of us, although I had a hunch she was only pretending to be surprised. She said, "Why, Tobey! You know you're supposed to be in bed by ten-thirty. And you're pretty young to be up so late, too, Brose. You'd better break it up before Mom finishes her package wrapping and discovers you're still around."

It is too simply degrading to be spoken to in that superior manner before the man you admire and to have the man you admire spoken to in that manner, too. But I hate vulgar brawls and I know Brose does, too. So both of us simply ignored her. We got up and I put our empty glasses and stuff on the sink and we left the room in complete dignity. I heard Alicia starting to open the refrigerator and I was glad we had eaten all the olives and left only a little squiggly piece of cake.

Brose said unhappily in the hall, "I suppose I'd better get going."

But I shook my head. "Don't give her the satisfaction."

Brose looked much happier at once. "Okay, I won't."

So we sat down on the hall stairs because from that vantage point we could hear anyone approaching from either the kitchen or the dining-room and Brose could grab his coat and leave by the front door and I could run upstairs without any further scoldings from anybody.

Brose said in a brooding sort of tone, "I think they're terrible to you, Tobey. Both your older sisters."

I sighed, and Brose picked up one of my hands and sat playing with my fingers, bending them back and forth.

18

"Oh, well," I moved my shoulders in a philosophical little shrug, "I guess sisters always get in each other's hair."

Brose is an only child, so he doesn't understand very well how it is with families. "But they pick on you so," he objected, "first Janet and then Alicia."

"They aren't always such blights," I told him. "Often they treat me quite decently. Alicia let me wear her velvet evening coat to the Junior Prom. And Janet pays me regular baby-sitter rates whenever I take care of Toots for her."

"You defend them," Brose said wonderingly. "You have a very noble nature, Tobey. I admire you for it. But—things won't always be this way for you. When I get older—"

He left it at that, sort of hanging in mid-air. But it was a very thrilling speech just the same. It implied wonderful things for the future, although one had to imagine just exactly what the things implied were.

He went on in a disgusted tone, "And that Adam Wentworth, standing there looking smug while Alicia called you down. You'd think he'd tell her where to get off."

"Tell Alicia where to get off?" I laughed hollowly. "He wouldn't dare."

"No, I don't s'pose so," Brose agreed. "And yet he thinks he's so much. He gives me a pain. The old Santa Claus—"

I stared at Brose blankly. The last part of his remark didn't make sense. "Santa Claus," I repeated.

Brose grinned. "Sure. Don't you know about that?"

I shook my head, still not getting it.

"You mean he hasn't even told Alicia?" Brose chuckled. "Not that I blame him much, at that. It is kind of ridiculous."

He went on to explain. Brose knew the details because his father is a buyer for Wentworth's Department Store and he had told them about it at home because it struck him sort of funny. The old man who played Santa Claus in the toy department had come down with tonsilitis a few days before. And Mr. Wentworth, who is pretty tight and suffers unreasonably over the amount of money Adam's medical education is costing him, had a brilliant idea. He decided that his son might as well help out, while he was at home for the Christmas holidays.

So Adam had been secretly spending his days at the store, wearing a red velvet suit and long white whiskers and a pillow from the bedding department stuffed in front to give him the proper figure. I remembered noticing that he hadn't been around so much lately except in the evenings. But in my wildest flight of fancy, I should never have suspected how he was occupying his time.

We sat there on the stairs when Brose had finished his recital, both of us rocking with laughter at the absurd thought of Adam in the role of Santa. But then I heard Mom and Dad emerging from the dining-room, so I gave Brose a warning push and he got up and hastily started getting into his overcoat.

"Why, darling, I thought—" Mom began and stopped. At least she was more tactful about telling me it was bedtime than Alicia had been.

"I'm just going, Mrs. Heydon," Brose said. "We got to talking and—well—the time just sort of—passed."

He smiled, a rather uncertain smile, and both Mom and Dad smiled back at him.

"Time," Dad said expansively, "practically always does."

"Yeah, doesn't it," Brose agreed politely. "Well—g'night, Mrs. Heydon—Mr. Heydon."

Mom and Dad said goodnight and I walked to the door with Brose. "I had a lovely time," I told him.

"So did I," Brose said. "G'night, Tobey. Be seeing you."

When the door had shut behind him, Mom said, "Such a nice boy."

She is really awfully sweet. I went over and put my arm around her and hugged her hard.

Dad yawned. "I'm exhausted," he said, rather as though the fact surprised him. "Wrapping all those packages, I suppose."

"No doubt, dear," Mom agreed, giving me a knowing, woman-to-woman look. She sighed, "I love Christmas, but I'll be almost glad when it's over. The closets are getting so dreadfully full. And there are still a million things I have to do."

"Well, it won't be long now," Dad said. He put his arm through hers and they started up the stairs.

"You must get to bed, too, Tobey," Mom said across her shoulder. "It's late."

"In just a sec," I promised.

I couldn't resist the temptation to go and stick my head into the kitchen and hiss, "Goodnight, Alicia—and Santa Claus."

Adam's back was toward me, but his neck got quite crimson, so I knew he had heard. And Alicia had caught my words, too, because as I turned away and scooted fast up the stairs after Mom and Dad, I heard my sister say, "Santa Claus? What on earth is she talking about, Adam?"

I didn't wait to hear his answer, although I was tempted to.

Chapter Three

'TWAS THE NIGHT BEFORE CHRISTMAS

$\mathcal{A}$licia was quite cool to me at breakfast. She looks ghastly in the morning, being so pale and washed-out without her make-up. Whereas both Janet and I have more color and can sparkle as effectively at the breakfast table as any other place.

Janet was trying to persuade Toots to eat his cereal instead of dropping it by spoonfuls into his orange juice, and Dad was reading the paper, and Midge was eating toast and licking the jam off of it, which is only one of her disgusting habits. Mother is always kept very busy mornings, making more toast and filling coffee cups and frying Dad's bacon and eggs just right. So she wasn't paying too much attention when Alicia addressed me frigidly.

"Tobey, when are you going to grow up and stop dressing like an absolute goon?"

23

I looked down at myself in surprise and then up questioningly at Alicia. I was very conservatively garbed in rolled-up blue jeans, white sox and loafers, a plaid flannel shirt with a white T-shirt underneath and my hair tied back with a red ribbon. There was absolutely nothing wrong with what I was wearing, so I knew Alicia was simply trying to pick a fight.

"What's your trouble?" I inquired reasonably. "Still mad about last night?"

Alicia glared at me. "I suppose you thought that was very funny—about Santa Claus."

I said nothing whatever, merely smiling inscrutably, which I know infuriates Alicia.

She went on, "Just because the regular Santa Claus developed a sore throat and Adam's father insisted that he dress up—"

Mother and Janet both said, "Shhh," very loud and Midge and Toots looked up interestedly and then all of a sudden Toots' face puckered up and he began to cry.

After much comforting and questions it turned out that he was crying because he figured if Santa Claus was sick with a sore throat he might not recover in time to bring the electric train which is all Toots has been talking or thinking about for some time. I think my father is looking forward to it, too.

Midge, who hasn't believed in Santa Claus for some time, spoke conversationally through a mouthful of cereal, "Lots of the kids at school think there isn't any Santa Claus."

This was a low blow on her part with Toots present. Mom exclaimed aghast, "Why, Midge, darling, haven't you written him a letter every single year? And hasn't he always brought you just what you wanted?"

Even Dad, who usually prefers to ignore his family at breakfast, stuck his head around the edge of his paper to eye Toots anxiously and put in, "Besides, that sore throat absolutely proves he's a real person. Hope he takes good care of himself, so he'll be all better by Christmas Eve."

Midge pretended to consider the matter judicially and Toots kept his eyes fixed unwaveringly on her face, as though he had decided to let his attitude be governed entirely by hers. Midge's jaws moved rhythmically as she chewed her toast and we all waited. The suspense was terrible. Finally she spoke.

"Well—I dunno. I guess there's a Santa Claus, all right. I hope he brings me some ice skates." Her gaze brightened hopefully as she asked Mom, "D'you s'pose he might?"

My mother said weakly, "Ice skates?" Midge had decided she wanted no less than ten different things during the past few weeks. "Well—he—he certainly won't bring them unless you believe he will. Why should he?"

Midge said craftily, "I'll b'lieve he will then," and went back to eating her toast.

Dad sort of choked behind his newspaper and Mom glared at him.

Toots said, beaming angelically around the table, "I b'lieve in him, too."

Janet proceeded to get the greater part of Toots's cereal down him. Then she and Mom encased him and Midge in their ski-suits and boots and mittens and sent them outdoors to play in the snow. At last we were able to talk and eat in peace.

My mother said, "Now what is all this about Adam and Santa Claus, Alicia? It was very thoughtless of you to speak as you did with Toots here."

"Well, I'm sorry," Alicia said. "I didn't think. But she makes me tired, and Adam didn't like it a bit."

She was glaring at me, so they all knew just who she meant. I glared right back at her.

Dad looked from Alicia to me over the top of his paper. "What's Tobey done now?"

Alicia proceeded to tell them all about it, the snitcher! "Just trying to embarrass Adam, that's what she was doing," she accused. "As if it were some sort of disgrace for him to play Santa Claus—and anyway, it's his father's doing. Mr. Wentworth simply insisted. And I think it's sweet of Adam," she finished, giving me a definitely dirty look.

I said pleasantly, "I think so, too. I can just see him with the lovely, darling, curly whiskers and the pillow in his tummy."

Janet grinned. "Why don't you have him come over Christmas Eve in costume and dispel any question our doubting Thomas might have implanted?" She indicated Midge's empty chair with a motion of her head. "It would thrill Toots to death."

I said, "Alicia, too. Think of being kissed by Santa Claus!"

But no one paid any attention to me.

My mother said raptly, her eyes shining with excitement, "Oh, Alicia, do you think he would? It would be such a treat for Toots. We'd have the tree all lit and Adam could come in by the window. Even Midge would enjoy it, although we'd have to tell her the truth beforehand. Do you suppose you could persuade Adam, Alicia?"

My sister seemed confident she could persuade Adam to do anything, up to arson or murder, so she promised to speak to him about it that very night. She tossed a gloating look in my direction and I knew she felt she had put me in my place, because no one else seemed to think it ridiculous for Adam to play Santa Claus. But it still struck me funny. And meeting my father's eye when no one else was looking, I caught his sly wink. So then I knew I wasn't alone in my amusement.

Alicia proved to be right in her estimation of her persuasive powers with Adam. Although he demurred strenuously at first and they argued about it all one evening, it was eventually settled that Adam would come in by the window and do his Santa Claus act for the children on Christmas Eve.

The last few days before Christmas are always pretty hectic at our house. This year they were especially so, since Midge was consumed with curiosity as to what she was going to get and troubled by few if any scruples about trying to find out. This necessitated our doing all wrapping and storing of gifts in the darkest secrecy, which meant after Toots and Midge had retired for the night. And even then, although Toots was fairly likely to stay put, one never knew when one would hear the childish patter of bare feet behind one and there would be Midge, bent on snooping.

But eventually Christmas Eve arrived. We were all pretty thrilled because no matter how blasé a person is normally, Christmas has a way of getting you just the same. This was especially true in my case, because I was naturally popping with curiosity over what else would be hidden in my package from Brose, along with the copy of *Ramona*. Then, too, I had done considerable hinting for a new formal and a taffeta housecoat and an argyle sweater with sox to match. And while I was hopeful, a girl can never be absolutely sure of anything, until she is throwing away the holly paper and tinsel ribbon after the gifts are unwrapped.

My mother is more reasonable than Mrs. Gilman, or maybe it is the mellowing influence of four daughters; anyway, she had allowed me to use my own judgment about a gift for Brose. I selected a perfectly wonderful fountain pen that will write in places where no normal person would think of writing. But Brose can use it in school and also later on when he goes away to college. When that time comes, the pen will serve to remind him of me, which will be a good thing as I am counting on his asking me to all the dances and football games.

Dinner on Christmas Eve is practically a waste of good

food in our house. No one ate much except Mom and Dad, who, I suppose, are too old to get very excited. Alicia was all jittery and could scarcely wait, because Adam was due via the window at seven-thirty. I could see Janet had been crying and I suppose it is sad to be away from the one you love on Christmas, especially after seeing a movie like *Tropic Love*. Jimmy hadn't even written her for several days. So no wonder she was feeling low.

But Toots and Midge were perfectly radiant and practically giving off sparks with joy. They scarcely touched their food, ignoring even dessert, which was ice cream. But nobody expected them to eat at such a time, not even Mom and Janet.

Midge was in on the secret about Adam, but Toots had merely been told that if he was very, very good, it was just possible that Santa might come before bedtime. Of course, all the rest of us knew that no matter how the children acted, Santa would put in his appearance at seven-thirty. Alicia had given him all sorts of instructions about being prompt and the ladder had been placed under the library window since five o'clock and all our presents were in a big bag made out of our old red drapes and hidden in the hall closet where Adam could get them easily. So there was no doubt whatever about Santa's arrival. Brose couldn't come over till a little later, since Adam had absolutely put his foot down and announced that if anyone other than the family was going to be there he, for one, would not!

When dinner was over, the children played around half-heartedly, their eyes absolutely glazed with expectancy, while we women got the dishes out of the way in a hurry. It's a wonder the poor clock didn't stop out of sheer contrariness, the way we all kept watching it and trying to push its hands ahead with our thoughts.

At seven-fifteen we adjourned to the library. There was a big fire blazing in the fireplace and all the lights were turned out except the bright colored bulbs on the tree. It was a big tree—Dad always saw to that. Every year Mom suggests, "Couldn't we have a sort of medium-sized tree this year, darling?" And every year Dad agrees, "Yes, sure. Size isn't important." And then he goes out and buys such a big one we always have to cut a couple of feet off the top to get it into the room. It looked lovely, though, with all the ornaments, some old and some new, and the ropes of tinsel and the silver icicles dripping down.

Midge and Toots hadn't seen it yet and their eyes got bigger than ever when they came into the room. They stood there, staring up at the tree, holding each other's hands. Even I had to admit that it was awfully exciting and sort of moving. There was such an ache in my throat that I could scarcely join in with the others when Mom started them off singing "Holy Night" and "Little Town of Bethlehem." Midge and Toots were absolutely thrilled silent, which was something new for them.

And then there came a soft, mysterious tapping on the window and the children jumped and I felt a little startled, because although I knew all the inner workings of the plan, it was certainly most effectively carried out.

Mom exclaimed, "Why—that must be Santa now!"

Dad went over and opened the window and Santa came in. I have to admit in all fairness that Adam made a very creditable figure in red velvet and curly white whiskers. Alicia had sneaked out into the hall when he was getting the bag of presents and had rouged his cheeks and the end of his nose and straightened his tummy for him. He looked like the real thing and if I had been ten years younger I could have believed, just as Toots obviously did, that he had just parked his sleigh and reindeer outside after zooming down from the North Pole.

Toots breathed, "Santa," over and over in an awed little voice. And Midge was getting a terrific kick out of being in on a secret with the grown-ups.

Adam spoke in a very gruff and Santa Clausish voice that no one could recognize as his own. He proceeded to distribute the gifts, saying, "Merry Christmas, Merry Christmas," and playing his part with fine fervor. I really didn't think Adam had it in him. Toots and Midge stood absolutely petrified, while Santa proceeded to stack their gifts in front of them. I think Midge actually forgot for a minute that he wasn't the real thing, or else she was simply so thrilled with Christmas she didn't care.

So then Adam went over to the window, beaming and saying, "Goodbye till next year. Be good, Merry Christmas."

Toots and Midge murmured, "Goodbye, Santa," and began to eye their stacks of gifts curiously.

Adam opened the window and sat on the sill and, with a last hearty wave, prepared to depart. Everything had gone absolutely according to plan up till now, but at this point things started being modified in a very decided and unforeseen manner. Santa swung his booted feet over the window sill onto the top of the ladder and suddenly the most peculiar expression broke over what was visible of his face between his whiskers and the furred edge of his peaked cap. And then he began frantically to wave his arms around in circles and with a muffled gasp of utter astonishment, he disappeared.

Chapter Four

BROSE SURPRISES ME

*F*ortunately Midge and Toots seemed to observe nothing amiss about the mode of Santa Claus' departure. They weren't paying any attention to him by that time, having fallen upon their gifts with whoops of delight. But all of us grown-ups stood absolutely dumbfounded for a moment. Then Alicia ran toward the window and the rest of us crowded after her. We were rewarded with a very surprising eyeful.

Just as the poem says, "The moon on the breast of the new-fallen snow gave a lustre of midday to objects below." But it wasn't any "miniature sleigh and eight tiny reindeer" which appeared to our wondering eyes. It took only a glance to see that Adam's abrupt disappearance had been due to the fact that the ladder had upset. And the ladder seemed to have upset because someone else had been occupying it at the moment of Adam's attempted departure. And now this someone was apparently all tangled up with Adam in the snow below.

Alicia, observing this, started to yell and when Alicia puts her mind on it she can yell in a most upsetting manner. Whether her yelling confused Adam still more, or whether the fall had knocked his innate intelligence out of him along with his breath, or whether, as seems most likely, it is just that the basic instinct of the male moves him, under such circumstances, to start fighting, we will never know. Anyway, that is what Adam started doing and this seemed to infuriate the person who was all tangled up with him and who had until now seemed fairly quiescent, and he started fighting, too.

This made Alicia scream still louder and now, as though there wasn't enough to bear without that, Janet suddenly started yelling, too. And I discovered to my intense surprise that Janet, who is usually a fairly controlled type of person, can yell even louder than Alicia.

All the noise seemed to galvanize my father into action. He sprinted for the front door. Mom went into action, too, but of a different nature. Midge and Toots, gradually becoming aware of the hullaballoo, were beginning to show signs of leaving their fascinating new toys and coming over to the window to investigate. But Mom, aware that one good look would shatter Toots's young illusions once and for all, managed to forestall them. She persuaded them to help her gather up Toots's electric stream-liner and the three of them took it into the living-room to start setting it up, although what Mom doesn't know about putting an electric train together would fill several volumes. Once she got them in there, she turned the radio on quite loudly and Bing Crosby's voice singing "White Christmas" helped drown out the noise my sisters were making.

Down below, the battle between Santa Claus and the mysterious stranger was in full sway, with snow flying in all directions and the stranger getting his mouth full of whiskers and Adam's pillow tummy falling out completely.

By this time Janet had begun to get faintly articulate and she pounded Alicia on the shoulder and shrieked, "Stop him, somebody! He'll kill him!"

Alicia wailed between belligerence and tears, "Who'll kill whom? Adam! Adam, can you hear me? Oh, my poor darling."

"Adam, stop it!" Janet yelled. "That's Jimmy." She entreated Alicia, "Can't you make him stop?"

Alicia was yelling, too. "You make Jimmy stop, why don't you?" For a minute it looked as though Janet and Alicia would really get into the spirit of the thing and start still another fight. But just then there was a sound of wheels turning onto our drive and a squeal of brakes and a car with EDGEWOOD POLICE printed on the side and someone hanging on the running board skidded to a halt.

By this time Dad had reached the scene of action and jumped into the middle of the melee, trying to pull the two furiously struggling figures apart. Now two police-men joined him and—my heart leaped!—none other than Brose, who had evidently been the figure hanging onto the running board.

Well, that was the beginning of the end. Between my father and Brose and the police it was just a matter of seconds till they got Adam and Jimmy pulled far enough apart so they could get a good look at each other.

So then Jimmy grinned through his cut lip and said, "Well, Santa Claus, as I live and breathe! I took you for a burglar."

"You took me for one?" Adam demanded, enraged still. "But that's what you are—sneaking up ladders—I could have broken my neck when I fell—"

"Boys, boys," my father laid a paternal hand on the shoulder of each. "I don't believe you two have met. Adam, this is Jimmy Clark, Janet's husband. And, Jimmy, this is Adam Wentworth, Alicia's fiancé."

Above the chorus of, "Darling, are you hurt badly?" and "Darling, how did you ever get here? I'll be right down," that Alicia and Janet were calling out the window, Brose's appalled voice was clearly audible.

"H-holy cow," he gulped, "then—m-maybe I shouldn't have gone for the police . . ."

Eventually it was all explained. Jimmy, who had ar-rived unannounced from Central America as a Christmas surprise for his family, had seen Adam's ladder standing under the window and thought it looked suspicious. So he put down his suitcase and climbed up the ladder stealthily, hoping to trap the intruder. And the next thing he knew, someone whom he took for an escaping house-breaker landed on top of him and the ladder upset with them both. Adam, apparently, was too mad to think at all when he was catapulted unexpectedly to the ground. Their starting to fight had been, as I suspected, purely reflex action.

In the meantime, Brose, who had been coming over to our house to bring me my present, had started up our front walk at the exact moment when Jimmy was sneaking stealthily over to climb the ladder and investigate. So naturally, he had immediately thought Jimmy was a burglar and had sped to summon the police.

Fortunately, our Edgewood police force seems to have a sense of humor. The two who had come to our assistance went off chuckling when Dad had given them each a handful of his Christmas cigars. Adam peeled out of his red velvet suit and whiskers before he came into the house, so Toots never was the wiser that it was he who had played Santa Claus. The version he got of the story was that Adam and Jimmy had happened to run into each other outside. Anyway Toots and Midge were too excited and thrilled over all their loot to pay much attention.

Alicia took Adam out into the kitchen and washed the blood off his nose and he was practically as good as new in no time. Jimmy didn't seem any the worse for his experience, either. He and Janet promptly took over the loveseat in the living-room. Before long Mom herded Midge and Toots up to bed over their fervent protests, and they would only go when she permitted Toots to take his electric train to bed and Midge her ice skates. Dad, who had got a new casting rod from Mom, slipped into the library where he could practice with privacy.

So that left Brose and me no place but the stairs, but we are so used to sitting on them we didn't mind at all. We hadn't given each other our gifts yet and the suspense was just about killing me, but still there was something I wanted to say to him before we began opening our respective packages.

"Brose," I told him, "I think you were simply wonderful tonight—really, I do."

"I don't see why." He sounded kind of embarrassed. "I guess it was pretty dopey of me going for the police, but I thought—"

"It wasn't dopey a bit," I interrupted firmly. "It was very quick thinking in an emergency. You showed initiative and sound judgment. Nine times out of ten it *would* have been a burglar sneaking up a ladder that way and not just my sister's husband. This just happened to be the tenth time, that's all."

"Yeah," Brose looked a little less crestfallen, "yeah, I guess so. At least, it's swell of you to figure that way, Tobey. I was kind of afraid at first that you might be mad at me—or that your Dad might."

"He wasn't at all," I assured him. "You heard him say he never got rid of his Christmas cigars so painlessly. And—I wasn't mad at you a speck, Brose. I admire you more than I can say."

38

"Gee, Tobey, do you really?" He picked up my hand and started playing with it, moving my fingers back and forth. "I—" he sort of gulped and got a little red, "I admire you very much, too. In fact, I think you're wonderful."

"Thank you, Brose." I looked down demurely at the package he had given me. The ribbon was tied kind of crooked, with one end trailing longer than the other, and one of the seals had come unstuck, so I was sure Brose had wrapped my gift himself. It gave me a nice warmish feeling, just thinking of it. I told him, "You look at your gift first. Go on, open it."

"Well, if you want me to." He undid the package and was very thrilled and pleased over his pen.

"You can use it," I told him, "even when you go away to college. Then you won't forget me."

"I wouldn't forget you ever, Tobey," Brose said earnestly. "Not at college or anywhere else—I couldn't."

"I'm glad," I told him.

I began unwrapping my parcel then. Sure enough, there was *Ramona* bound in leather, just as Brose had warned me. But underneath, wrapped separately in tissue paper, were two other little packages. I opened them, my heart palpitating.

Brose is too, too sweet! Guess what else he gave me besides *Ramona!* A bottle of My Sin perfume and a lipstick which is a much darker shade than Janet's and she can keep hers after this for all I care.

"Oh, Brose," I said softly. I couldn't seem to say anything else, just that. "Oh, Brose . . ."

He took both my hands in his and leaned quite close to me, there on the stairs. And it seemed like the least I could do under the circumstances was to give him a little kiss. It was the first time I had done so. But I had always suspected Brose would be very nice to kiss. And he was.

Chapter Five

THE WONDERFUL WEEK

$\mathcal{I}$ simply love holiday week. It is always filled with such wonderful excitement, building up thrillingly to the climax of New Year's Eve. And this year it all seemed more marvelous than ever before. There was something doing every minute, sleigh rides, dances, skating parties on Lake Ellen, with refreshments afterwards at someone's house. Brose and I were in on the whole merry whirl that involved our particular crowd. Alicia and Adam and Janet and Jimmy took part in the doings of all their friends. Midge's crowd of young fry were active in their own childish way. And even Mom and Dad seemed to be kept pretty much on the go with their more staid amusements.

Then on New Year's Eve we had a big party at our house. I can't even remember how many people stopped in during the course of that very gay evening, some staying a little while, others lingering for hours and hours. Dad had rolled up the library rug, so we used that room exclusively for dancing. Some of the older couples played cards in the living-room. Lots of people just drifted around from one room to another, kibitzing the bridge games and watching us younger people dance. There was so much talk and laughter it was almost deafening. Along toward morning we all had bacon and scrambled eggs and coffee and doughnuts, and that sort of wound things up. People began going home after that and everyone said they had a simply terrif time. Barbie Walters, who is my very dearest friend and on whom I can always depend to tell me the absolutely unvarnished truth, said it was the most perfectly wonderful party she had ever attended. So I guess it was a success all right.

I don't know why it is that parties are always so hard on older people. We all slept late the next morning, except Janet, who had to get up at the crack of dawn with Toots as usual. I felt perfectly wonderful and ready for anything at breakfast. But even with all that sleep, Mom and Dad looked sort of wan and weary.

"I have always felt," Dad said, toying with his waffle in a way not at all like himself, "that it would be a great improvement if there was a holiday called Day-For-Getting-Over-New-Year's-Eve. It could be sandwiched in between New Year's Eve and New Year's Day with very little trouble. I think I'll write my congressman."

Poor Dad didn't even seem to be enjoying his coffee.

42

He kept holding his water glass against his forehead and shutting his eyes, as though the sight of his assembled family, even at almost eleven o'clock in the morning, was more than he could bear. But it was really much calmer than usual around our table. Midge and Toots were outdoors playing, Janet and Jimmy seemed sort of quiet and preoccupied, and even Alicia and I hadn't had a word of disagreement since we sat down to our meal. Secretly, I had made a New Year's resolution to try to get along a little better with Alicia. Maybe she had some such idea, too.

Mom said faintly, "It wouldn't be so bad if only people wouldn't always have Open Houses on New Year's Day. We're supposed to put in an appearance at five at least—" she broke off, frowning. "I *think* it was just five invitations I definitely accepted."

"The appearance I put in," Dad said in a sort of low moan, "will not be my best, I assure you. At the moment I do not feel equal to looking even one eggnog in the eye, let alone five."

Mom said, "Oh, dear," as though she hadn't thought of the eggnogs that went with the Open Houses till that minute.

After that, conversation lagged. Alicia seemed to be thinking of Adam, at least she had that limpid-eyed, dreamy sort of expression. Maybe I had it, too, because I was certainly thinking of Brose. He had been so wonderful last night and even more handsome than usual in a new plaid sport jacket he had got for Christmas. And he was coming over, and we were going for a long walk this afternoon. Somehow, going for a long walk with Brose seemed like a wonderful way to start the new year. The mere thought of it made me feel all soft and quivery inside.

Suddenly Janet's voice broke into my pleasant abstraction, but not her usual voice. She sounded all sort of keyed up and tense exclaiming, "Jimmy, I'm simply going to have to ask them! I can't stand it another minute!"

Jimmy said seriously, "Baby, are you sure it's what you want to do?"

All of us stared from one of them to the other a bit blankly. Janet nodded her head in a very positive manner, so that her dark red hair bobbed against the sides of her neck.

"I'm sure, darling. I want it more than anything in the world. And—I don't think Mom and Dad will mind dreadfully when they know how I feel about it."

Dad had taken his water glass away from his forehead to look at her more directly. "Would you mind telling us what you're talking about?"

My mother, who is quite a remarkable woman in some ways, said calmly, smiling a little, "I know what she's talking about. You want to go back with Jimmy when he leaves on Wednesday, don't you, Janet? You want Toots to stay with us for a while."

"Oh, yes," Janet breathed, her eyes fixed almost prayerfully on Mom's face. "That's exactly what I want to do. I simply can't stand it any longer having Jimmy thousands and thousands of miles away. And yet I know the climate down there would be awful for Toots—I simply couldn't take him. But Jimmy feels it would be too much of an imposition, dumping Toots on you—and I suppose it would, really—but, oh, Mom—" Her voice sort of broke.

"I know, dear," Mom soothed. "I know just how you feel."

Jimmy said uncomfortably, "I thought it would be better if we could be together even for a little while— that's why I got this leave of absence to come up, but—" His voice ran down.

"But it didn't help, did it?" Mom said gently. She was looking at Janet and Janet was looking at her. "You've been miserable and lonely for months. It was easy to see. And being with Jimmy again has made it worse instead of better. After you've had these few days together, you simply can't face the thought of his going away again and leaving you."

Janet nodded and her eyes got very bright, as though she might be going to cry. She said, "Oh, Mom—you're wonderful! You do understand."

"Of course I understand. And so does your father. Don't you, Henry?"

Dad looked a little dazed. "Well, yes—I understand, all right. But, Laura—" he looked very straight at my mother, "are you sure?"

"Of course, I'm sure," Mom told him. She addressed Janet and Jimmy then, "You two should be together. It's only right and natural. And since Jimmy's job happens to be in a place that wouldn't be good for Toots, we'll be very happy to keep him for you. And it won't be any imposition, either, so you just get such a thought right out of your minds."

"Gee, Mom—Dad—" Jimmy said sort of huskily, "you're swell, both of you. I'm luckier than I deserve, marrying into a family like yours."

"The family," Dad said, "is a wonderful institution. Families should stand together, help each other out, be there to depend on. I'd love to have Toots stay with us, so long as Laura doesn't feel it'll be too much for her. After all, she's not as—"

"Henry Heydon!" Mom exclaimed warningly. "Don't you dare say I'm not so young as I once was! Besides, if I could cope with four girls, I guess one little boy won't be too much for me."

"True," Dad agreed. "And look at all the help you'll have—Alicia and Tobey, even Midge."

"Sure," I said, feeling a little dazzled by the way Janet and Jimmy were looking at each other.

I guess Alicia must have been thrilled by that look, too, because she said, "Of course, we'll help. We'll be glad to."

Mom smiled at us. "If four able-bodied females and one doting grandfather can't take care of Toots, it'll be just too bad."

Jimmy told us all, "It won't be for any longer than I can help, I promise you. I expect to be sent out to California in a couple of months and we'll certainly want Toots with us then."

Janet said, "You're all being so perfectly wonderful about it, I could just cry."

"You haven't time," Mom told her sensibly. "You have a thousand things to do—packing, and tomorrow you'll have to shop for some summer clothes. It's hot where you're going and Wednesday's only two days off."

"Golly!" Janet exclaimed, wide-eyed, starting to push back her chair. "That's right!"

"I think," Dad told her dryly, "you'll have time to finish your breakfast."

So it was all settled that Janet was to go to Central America with Jimmy, and Toots was to stay with us, just like that. I guess my mother and father are pretty wonderful, any way you look at it . . .

After all that excitement at breakfast, I sort of expected the rest of New Year's Day would turn out to be pretty calm. But I was mistaken. The most wonderful and exciting thing of all happened that afternoon when Brose and I went for our long walk.

It was a lovely day, fairly cold but clear and bright, so that the sky looked impossibly blue and the snow impossibly white, and all the trees and houses and things had a clear-cut sort of look, as though they had been cut out and pasted on. It was like walking through a Christmas card scene instead of a real one. And maybe the fact that we seemed to have the world pretty much to ourselves added to that illusion. I guess nobody else thought about going for a long walk on New Year's, but I was awfully glad that we had.

47

Brose had on a leather jacket and brown corduroy pants and his red earmuffs and big flapping galoshes. I wore my green gabardine ski suit and my bunny fur earmuffs and mittens and my lambskin-lined boots. So we were both snug and warm and felt like walking forever. We went down the road that goes around the east edge of Lake Ellen, where a lot of people were skating. Their voices came to us clear and sort of musical through the stillness. After a while we left the lake shore, and then pretty soon we couldn't hear the voices anymore. The houses got fewer and fewer and before long we were out in the country. There was an old-fashioned rail fence sticking up through the snow, and we floundered through a deep drift in order to sit on it and rest for a while before starting back toward town.

I had told Brose all about Janet and Jimmy and about our going to keep Toots for them. We had talked about ever so many things as we walked, but now, sitting close together on the old rail fence, our conversation seemed to have sort of run down. Not that we minded. We are not the sort of friends who have to go yah-tah-tah yah-tah-tah all the time, talking and talking in order to keep from being bored. I think there is a deeper kind of understanding between us than many people have, even older people than we are.

Somewhere far off a train whistle cried, and it was such a lonely sound I felt sorry for it. Just hearing it made me feel a little lonely, too, till Brose reached out and pulled off one of my mittens and held my hand close and warm in his. Then I felt wonderful.

Brose said, "Tobey."

"Yes?"

"I—well, I don't quite know how to say this. I guess I never felt like saying it to any girl before—but—well, I like you an awful lot."

My heart beat so fast it felt smothery. "I like you very much, too, Brose."

"Better than any other boy?"

I thought about it for a minute, although it really didn't need much thinking about. But I wanted to be honest, perfectly honest. "Better than any boy I've ever met."

Brose let out his breath in a sort of relieved way. "That's just how I feel about you," he told me.

"I'm glad."

We sat there for quite a while then, not saying anything, our shoulders touching and our hands clasped tight together.

When Brose spoke again his voice was all husky and his expression solemn. "Tobey, do you like me well enough to take a very serious step?"

My heart bumped hard. "What do you mean?"

"My class ring," Brose said hoarsely. "Would you wear my class ring, Tobey?"

I frowned. "But, Brose, you don't have it yet."

At Edgewood High you don't get your class ring till you're a Senior. And neither Brose nor I would be Seniors till next September.

49

"No, of course not," Brose said. "But will you wear it when I do get it?"

Nothing quite so wonderful had ever happened to me in my whole entire life. I just sat there, looking up at him. My eyes must have glowed like stars—at least, they felt as if they were glowing like stars. I gasped, "Why—why—"

"Will you, Tobey?" Brose insisted solemnly.

"Well—yes, I think so, Brose—only—just what does it mean to wear a boy's class ring? It isn't being really engaged, is it?"

"Not exactly, I guess." Brose sounded a little doubtful, as though he wasn't too sure what it meant himself. "I guess we're a little young to get really engaged—but I like you so much—"

I nodded. I felt that way, too. I told him, "If wearing your ring will mean we're very *best* friends—and that I like going with you more than any other boy I know, then I'd love to wear it, Brose—when you get it next fall, that is."

His face lit up. "Gee, will you? That'll be swell."

A thought struck me—a terrible thought. "But—what if we both don't feel like this about each other then? It's a long time."

"Oh, we will," Brose said confidently. "At least, I will. And I hope you will, too."

He sounded so terribly serious I couldn't help laughing. So then he laughed, too, and suddenly we both seemed to feel the same urge. We jumped down from the old rail fence and floundered through the snow drift toward the road. I couldn't resist the temptation to make a big squashy snowball and throw it at Brose across my shoulder. So then he had to go a step further and wash my face with an icy cold handful of snow. The stinker!

It was a perfectly wonderful New Year's Day.

Chapter Six

A FAVOR FOR JANET

$\mathcal{T}$he next couple of days passed so fast it made us all sort of dizzy. Janet was in such a rush getting ready to fly south with Jimmy on Wednesday. There was shopping to do and packing, a hundred last-minute instructions about Toots's care and schedule, as if Mom didn't know as much about that as Janet did. But I guess the closer it got to time for her to actually leave her child, the more panic-stricken Janet became at the prospect. Her maternal instinct was outraged at the thought of going off without Toots and her wifely love wouldn't let her think of Jimmy's going off without her. She was really on a spot. Toots was by far the calmest person around our house. He wasn't at all concerned about his Mommy's leaving with his Daddy, as long as he got to stay with Grandma and Grandpa—and his new electric train. Children are such realists.

The night before she left Janet came into my room when I was getting ready for bed. She looked sort of desperate. I was brushing my hair and she curled up on the foot of my bed in her quilted house-coat and fixed me with a definitely worried glance.

"Tobey," she said, "the most awful thought just occurred to me. I don't know why I didn't think of it sooner."

"Ninety-eight, ninety-nine, a hundred," I counted my brush strokes and then paused, expectantly. "What thought is that?"

Janet continued to sit there on my bed, her arms clasped around her knees, looking stricken. "It's about Toots."

"Natch. But what about Toots?" I didn't mean to sound callous, but really Janet had been in such a dither the past twenty-four hours I was beginning to lose patience. "After all, you have to make up your mind. Either you must trust Mom to take care of him or—"

"Oh, it's not that I don't trust her," Janet broke in. "I know she'll take wonderful care of him—only—well, it's just this. I'll be away off down there in the wilds of Central America, and I'll want to hear often how Toots is getting along. And you know how Mom is about writing letters," she finished in a sort of wail.

I got her point at once. My mother is a woman of sterling character and many worthy accomplishments, but letter writing is not her long suit. She can think of more excuses to put off answering her mail than anyone else

I know, being practically allergic to pen and ink. For one thing, she is pretty busy, and she was going to be busier than ever with Toots to take care of. Any way you looked at it, I saw what a vicious circle the whole business must appear to Janet.

"I see what you mean," I said thoughtfully.

And Janet moaned, "Weeks—months!—may pass without my getting a letter from Mom."

"She could always send you a wire if anything of a drastic nature came up," I pointed out.

"Don't talk like that! Naturally, I'm not figuring on anything drastic happening. It's just that I'd feel so much easier in my mind if I could count on hearing from someone in the family, say, once a week." The way she sat there, looking so straight at me when she said that, put her idea over pretty clearly.

"Huh-uh!" I said flatly. "You're not going to pin me down to any rash promise like that! I'm not too crazy about writing letters, either. Once a week—gosh!"

"Suppose there was money in it for you?" Janet regarded me narrowly. "You're always bewailing the fact you can't make your allowance stretch to cover your expenses."

"Money," I repeated, "for writing letters?"

It was an intriguing thought. And it is perfectly true that in this period of high prices, even for simple little pleasures like movies and double chocolate nut sundaes, an allowance the size of mine is, to say the least, inadequate. But the last time I broached this subject to my father, he gave me such a sad story of the way his income had failed to keep up with the rising cost of living and of how hard it was nowadays to support a large family that I ended up feeling maybe I ought to lend him money. My personal finances are always in a mad snarl and Janet couldn't have hit upon a better way to catch my interest and insure my co-operation.

She nodded, a little smile playing around her mouth, as though she remembered how it used to be when she was my age and practically always broke. "Sure," she said. "I'm perfectly willing to pay you, say, a dollar a week, if I can count on you to write me a letter that often and let me know how Toots is getting along."

"A dollar a week," I said brightly. That is the equivalent of two movies, or four sundaes, or ever so many other luxuries I could think of. "Say, you got yourself a correspondent. For that I'll promise to write you a nice long newsy letter once a week about your child."

"Good!" Janet beamed. She hopped off my bed and thrusting her hand into her housecoat pocket brought out two one dollar bills. "Here's for a couple of weeks in advance. And you're sure I can count on you?"

"To the death," I assured her. I took the bills and then a sudden arresting thought occurred to me. "Uh—Janet."

"Yes?"

"You won't mention this arrangement to Mom, will you? She—well, she might think it was a little bit mercenary of me."

"I won't tell her." Janet gave me a little hug and moved

toward the door. "You and I know it is purely a matter of business. And thanks a lot, Tobey. You've taken a load off my mind."

"That's okay. I'll start writing just as soon as you've had time to get there . . ."

Janet and Jimmy got off all right the next morning. They took the train to Chicago and a southbound plane from there. Two days later their wire came saying they had arrived safely. I figured that was my cue to sit down and write Janet a long reassuring letter about Toots. I am nothing if not a woman of my word—besides, there was money involved in this deal and that, I felt, made my obligation even more binding. But somehow it is rather hard to write to a person you have seen and talked with as recently as I had seen and talked with Janet. She knew everything that had been going on around our house up to the moment of her departure only a couple of days before. There really wasn't any news I could pass along. So I wrote her that Toots was doing fine, that we were all well, that it had snowed some more, that school would be starting in a few more days and that I was *not* looking forward to it. I told her I'd write in more detail next time and let it go at that. And then, because I was feeling a little guilty about the letter being only one page long, I walked down to the post office and sent it air-mail, just to ease my conscience.

Really, I admonished myself severely, I would have to do better than this, or I wouldn't be earning my dollar a week.

But, sure enough, by the time I owed Janet another letter quite a few things had happened for me to relate. I figured I should tell her all the news and not merely how Toots was getting along. Because after all, she would no doubt be interested in hearing what was happening to the rest of the family, too. So I wrote her a long, detailed account of things in general, almost as long an account as I usually write in my diary.

The letter went as follows:

Dear Janet:

Just to relieve your mind at the very beginning, Toots is in excellent health and no more trouble than usual. After all, Mom says you can't expect too much of a boy of three when grown-up people who ought to have more sense act the way this family does. But you know how Mom talks. She doesn't really think we're so bad. Nevertheless, Janet, she has been pretty busy since you left, what with riding herd on Toots and getting Midge started back to school and one thing and another. So I doubt she's had time to write you even one letter. And isn't it a good thing you were foresighted enough to make this arrangement with me? Otherwise, who can say how much time might elapse before you heard how your child was doing. This way you needn't ever have an anxious moment, as you know how perfectly dependable I am and much older than my years in many ways, don't you think?

I am back in high school again, and it all seems sort of dull and boring after all the fun that went on during the holidays. Not too dull and boring, of course, and I will probably get used to it again before long and not even remember what I'm missing. It must be wonderful, though, to be entirely grown-up like you and not have to go to school any more and I am surely looking forward to it.

Well, how do you like it down there where you are? Is it like that movie "Tropic Love" with lots of smouldering and dangerous native girls on the loose and all the American engineers disintegrating? I think myself that the disintegration must have been a little exaggerated, because when Jimmy was here Christmas, he seemed the same as ever only more sunburned.

We are all well, only Alicia, and I don't mean she is sick, but Adam has gone back to college and I guess it is pretty hard on an engaged girl when she can't see her fiancé very often. She has been sort of mooning around like a lost soul ever since Adam left, but she has begun to perk up again the last day or so because tomorrow is Saturday and he is coming back to Edgewood for the weekend. And then next week his fraternity is giving their big winter dance, and Alicia is going up to the university for that. She has the most absolutely super new formal for the occasion, Janet, and honestly does it seem fair to you? Because that swish black net of hers is still perfectly good, while I haven't had a new formal since that ghastly old yellow rag I got for the Junior Prom and it is six months old if it is a day and I look like nothing human in it. And I am going to have to wear it for the Hi-Y dance to which Brose Gilman has invited me next week. But, of course,

Brose's is just a high-school club and I am just me, so when I broached the subject of a new dress to Mom in a perfectly reasonable way, she merely said, "Hush, darling. I can't ask Daddy to provide any more clothes for anybody till Spring at the very earliest. If you'd heard what he said about Alicia's—"

I said, "I did hear—being in the house at the time."

So then Mom went on with that line about it being too soon after the holidays to incur any unnecessary expenses.

I couldn't help feeling a little hurt by her attitude, so I said with quiet dignity, "Alicia being the only one who isn't affected by all this economizing?"

Mom didn't think it was very nice of me to talk so. She said, "Tobey, surely you're old enough to understand. Alicia is engaged to be married to Adam. Naturally, when she's going up to his college, she wants to look her very best. Besides, your yellow dress is simply lovely on you, so sweet and girlish. And after all, you've only worn it once."

How can older people, even mothers, be so absolutely lacking in understanding, Janet? I knew it would be a waste of time to continue the argument, so I accepted defeat gracefully. But I couldn't help thinking: Don't you suppose I want to look my best, as well as Alicia? And as for being engaged—well, I practically am, too.

This is a secret, Janet, and you must not refer to it in any of your letters, because it would be murder if it were ever found out. But Brose and I practically almost are engaged. New Year's Day he asked me if I would wear his class ring next fall when he gets it. And I said I would, provided we both felt the same way about each other as we do now. And you know what a class ring means—not quite an engagement but the very next thing to it. Because I am almost certain that we will still feel the same way next fall—ours is the sort of feeling that goes on and on, I feel sure. And when I am with Brose, I feel all sort of warm and quivery and unsettled inside and if that isn't evidence of a very deep feeling, I don't know what it is. Did Jimmy affect you that way, Janet? Before you were married, I mean?

Anyway, to get back to my clothes problem, I got one break. Brose's club dance falls on the same Saturday night as the fraternity dance at the university. And, of course, Alicia will only take along her new dress and I have a confident hunch that once she is safely gone for the week-end, I can work on Mom and get her to let me wear Alicia's black net. None of my friends have seen it, due to Alicia's going around with an older crowd, so it would be just as good as a new formal for me. I would ask Alicia herself to let me wear it, but you know how stingy she is about her clothes. So I think Mom will be my best bet.

Well, I will close for this time, because I have just heard a loud scream from behind the garage where Midge and Toots are playing. Knowing my sister as I do, I suspect she has been up to something and Toots is probably the victim. I am supposed to be watching them while

Mom does the marketing, so I will go out and investigate now. I do not think it is serious, though, because Toots always yells louder when he is mad than when he is hurt. And he is yelling very loud indeed right now.

With love,
Tobey

P.S. I have already written up the two dollars worth you paid me in advance before you left. So please send along another payment for some more reports on Toots. He has already quit crying, so you needn't worry about him a bit. He is fine and I will write you a long letter just like this every week, so you won't have a minute's uneasiness about him. Isn't it wonderful we thought of this arrangement?

As ever,
Tobey

Chapter Seven

I SCHEME A SCHEME

*I*t was lucky I got that long letter about Toots off to Janet when I did, because things went very haywire around our house the next few days and I didn't have much time for writing. All in the space of one little week-end the whole shape of the future altered in a way that I for one found most disconcerting. Almost before I was able to grasp what was happening, the fraternity dance to which Alicia had planned to go with Adam, was all off. Everything was all off! Personally, I think Alicia is nuts to pick a time like that to have a big fight with her fiancé. After all, it is better to use a little judgment and common sense. If a couple simply has to scrap, they can pick another time than right before a big important date. But not Adam and Alicia! They have to be spectacular.

1 SCHEME A SCHEME

Adam came down from college on Saturday for the week-end, just as I had written Janet he intended to do. Alicia greeted him joyfully and everything was apparently lovely up to the time that Brose and I left for Barbie Walters' house Sunday night. She had Sox Trevor, her special heart-throb, over, too. The four of us had a super time and her mother gave us malteds and chocolate cake for refreshments. And Brose and I walked home the long way 'round. I said goodnight to him at the door, because Mom and Dad are adamant about my getting to bed by ten-thirty when I have to go to school the next morning. When I had hung my things in the hall closet, I stuck my head into the living-room where my parents were listening to sentimental music on the radio and glancing through the tag-end of the Sunday paper.

They glanced up and Mom said approvingly, "I'm glad you got in early, dear. Alicia's home early, too. She went right on upstairs without even stopping to say goodnight. I guess she was thinking about Adam."

"No doubt," I agreed. Still it struck me as rather odd for Alicia to get home this early from a date with Adam.

Mom said, "You'd better get to bed, Tobey. Didn't you mention something about having a test at school tomorrow?"

It was in Physics, I recalled with no enthusiasm. "Why remind me of it?"

"Let her be happy while she may," Dad chanted from behind his paper. "Come tomorrow, she won't feel gay."

I sometimes think there must have been a thwarted poet,

to use the term loosely, in Dad's ancestry and that it left a mark on him. He has a weakness for corny jingles.

"Ouch," I said. "I'll go to bed before you can think up anything else like that to spring on me. G'night, parents."

I proceeded to go upstairs. Scarcely had I reached the top when the sound of stormy sobbing from Alicia's room smote my ears. I suppose the only reason Mom and Dad hadn't heard her was because the radio was on. Naturally, I decided to investigate. There was just a possibility that Alicia might be ill from all the shrimp salad she had eaten for supper. But that wasn't it. I could tell the minute I got into her room and saw her lying face down on her bed crying into her pillow that she was mad, not sick. And my heart fell as I realized she must be mad at Adam.

"Alicia," I sat down beside her and laid a comforting hand on her shoulder, "what's the matter?"

"Go away," she moaned in a muffled voice. "Leave me alone."

Discouraging as her attitude was, I was too curious about what had happened to give up so easily. "But what's wrong?"

"Everything," Alicia gulped. "Simply everything. Men are so awful, I hate every single one of them. Especially Adam," she wailed. And then she added, "Not that it's any of your business."

That's my sister, always about as confidential as a clam. I never did find out exactly what had happened, probably very little, since I have realized for a long time that it doesn't take much to precipitate a quarrel between Alicia and Adam. They can fight harder and make up with more enthusiasm than any other couple I know. Sometimes I actually think they enjoy their emotional upheavals, or maybe it's all just a part of being madly in love.

Anyway, Alicia insisted that everything was over between them and that she had returned his fraternity pin and never wanted to see him again—never, never! Of course, I knew this was a lot of hooey and that she would just naturally curl up her toes and die if she never saw him again. But I didn't say so, being tactful by nature. Instead, I consoled her to the best of my ability and got a cool damp cloth from the bathroom to wash her face.

I couldn't help thinking how terrible she looked, with her eyes all red and puffy and her hair mussed up. Honestly, I hope she won't cry every time she gets mad at Adam after they are married, because she always looks like the end of a misspent life when she cries and I should think it would be very disillusioning for a young husband.

I felt confident they would make up eventually. They always do. But I crossed my fingers mentally and hoped it would be before Saturday. Alicia would be crazy if she stayed mad at Adam long enough to miss that wonderful dance. Sometimes it seems to me that although she is several years my senior, she hasn't nearly as sound judgment as I have. Anyway, it was important to me personally this time for her not to be too stubborn and stiff-necked about making up with Adam. I had toyed with the idea of wearing her black net formal to the Hi-Y dance too long to give up the plan without a struggle. And knowing Alicia, I realized she could be just mean enough not to let me wear it, even if she wasn't using it herself. There is a little sadistic streak in my sister that makes her want to see everybody else suffer whenever she is unhappy.

I went to sleep that night with a good deal more than a test in Physics weighing on my mind . . .

Monday and Tuesday dragged past in the most utterly appalling fashion. I got through my test by a very narrow margin, which wasn't surprising considering that Physics is not my best subject and that I had much more vital and important things to think about.

Walking me home from school Tuesday afternoon, even Brose, who is not always too observant, noticed that I was jittery and abstracted. He inquired sympathetically, "What's eating you?"

I am not one to confide my family's private affairs to outsiders, but Brose is such a close friend. So I told him about Alicia's bitter quarrel with Adam.

"This is news?" Brose inquired. "I thought those two were always having scraps and making up again and having more scraps."

"Well, they are," I admitted. "But this one is a dilly, even for them. It's been two days now and Adam hasn't even called up."

"Oh, well," Brose shrugged, "they'll get over it. Anyway, since when have you taken to worrying over Alicia's love life?"

I didn't want to go into all the details about my yearning to wear her black formal. For one thing, I wanted to dazzle Brose with it, if I was lucky enough to get to wear it. And for another thing, with the present unsettled state of affairs, it looked as though I'd have to wear my old yellow dress after all, so there was no use building up his expectations. Besides, men never seem to understand the importance of problems involving clothes, so I doubted whether he would be properly sympathetic.

So I merely said enigmatically, "Blood is thicker than water. After all, I don't like to see my own sister unhappy, even if I don't always get along so well with her myself." Then I guided the conversation into other channels and the rest of our walk home was taken up with a discussion of various inconsequential subjects.

When still another day passed with no phone call from Adam, I began to feel almost as low as Alicia. I toyed with the idea of suggesting that she call him, but I knew this would be a complete waste of breath, since Alicia was by this time as proud and stubborn about the whole business as she was mad.

Wednesday night Mom and Dad decided to go to the movies. They left in time for the first show, and I put Toots to bed soon after their departure. He is always pretty tired by seven o'clock, having been going strong from practically the crack of dawn when he arises. Midge went less willingly, but I had her settled without too much difficulty by eight o'clock. Then I went downstairs to the library, where Alicia was curled up morosely on the davenport, listening to a mystery thriller on the radio.

Or maybe she wasn't really listening to it, but at least she had it turned on. It sounded pretty good, too, so I flopped down in a comfortable chair and started to give it my full attention.

Just at the most interesting part, natch, there was a sound of car wheels on our drive, followed by the noise of a car door opening and slamming. Alicia jumped up and flew to the window, and then she sort of seemed to freeze up, although I could see that she was a little gratified, too.

She said dramatically, "It's Adam! Tobey, I won't see him. You must go to the door and tell him I have nothing whatever to say to him."

I answered, "Nuts!" which may have been inelegant, but it certainly expressed my feelings. Honestly, sometimes it seems to me Alicia hasn't the sense she was born with. "You can't treat him like that when he's driven all the way down from college to see you. Why, it's seventy-five miles each way! And he'll have to get back by midnight. You haven't any time to waste."

"I won't see him," she insisted, "after the way he's treated me."

"You haven't treated him very well, either," I argued. "Don't be a dope! Go powder your nose, and I'll let him in for you."

But Alicia repeated, "No, I'm not going to see him."

She started fluffing her hair out around her face, though, which I took as an encouraging sign.

The door-bell rang then and Alicia just stood there.

68

So I went to the door and there was Adam, looking sort of apologetic and miserable. I really felt sorry for him, even if he does usually infuriate me by treating me like a child.

I said, quite loudly, because I knew darned well Alicia would be listening, even though she had closed the library door behind me, "Oh, hello, Adam. This is a surprise!"

And Adam gulped and his eyes looked awfully unhappy, and he had always been so sort of nonchalant and superior with me before that it seemed terrible to see him so humbled. And he asked, "Is Alicia home, Tobey? I want to see her."

And I said, still loud for Alicia's benefit, because an idea was beginning to form in my mind, due to a movie I had seen a while back, "Oh, she's home, Adam. But she won't see you. She has nothing to say to you." And then I stood on my tiptoes so I could whisper in his ear, "Go on in the library and make her listen to you, whether she wants to or not! Don't be a worm. Treat her rough, Adam, and make her like it!"

He gasped and then his eyes brightened a little and he whispered back, "Do you—suppose she would?"

And I nodded real hard right while I was saying aloud, "I'm sorry, Adam, but I'm afraid it's no use."

So then he started moving sort of hesitantly toward the library. And I made a scuffling noise with my feet, as if he had shoved me masterfully out of his way, and I gave him a little push from behind, too, so he'd go in there more purposefully and as though he would brook no nonsense.

I heard Alicia gasp as the door swung open and then Adam said sort of chokingly, "Alicia—you've got to listen to me—"

They forgot to shut the door and while I wouldn't for a minute listen through a closed door, I don't really consider it eavesdropping to simply stand in the hall of one's own home, even if a supposed-to-be-private conversation is going on in an adjoining room.

So I just stood there and Alicia said, "I told you it was no use, Adam," very coolly and regally. "We said everything we had to say to each other Sunday night. You might as well have saved yourself the trouble of driving down."

I was scared for a minute that Adam was just going to take her high-handed treatment, as he had got in the habit of doing, and not remember the good advice I had given him. But then I heard him cross the room toward her with what sounded like masterful strides. And I guess, he must have grabbed Alicia and started kissing her. But he must not have done it so well as the hero of the movie, because Alicia, unlike the heroine, did not succumb to his caveman tactics at all.

I could hear what sounded like a struggle, climaxed by a sharp slap. And then Alicia's voice, positively dripping icicles, said, "Adam Wentworth, don't you dare treat me like that! I won't stand for it, do you hear? You—you brute! Oh, I hate you!"

And then she came hurrying out of the room and up the stairs, throwing me a very dirty look indeed as she realized

I must have heard everything. Then Adam rushed out, too, but not after Alicia. He gave me an even dirtier look than she had and I noticed that one of his cheeks was much redder than the other as he strode past me toward the front door.

However, I could not feel that I was to blame for the way things had worked out. My advice had been given with the very best intentions, since my interest in Alicia's going to the dance with Adam was as great as his own if not greater. And when he slammed out of the house, I felt desperate, because I knew from experience the utter impossibility of trying to reason with my sister.

Instinctively I grabbed my coat from the closet and hurried out after Adam. He was just starting the car when I hopped on the running-board and naturally he couldn't shove me off.

So he merely said in a terrible tone, "Well, what now, Scourge?"

I don't think this was a nice way to speak to me and some more appropriate time I will get even with him. Now I merely climbed in beside him and said pleadingly, "Don't be mad at me, Adam. I was just trying to help you. Maybe we can think of something else."

Adam said, "Hah!" in a loud insulting tone.

But I ignored this, merely saying meekly, "You see, I—I like you so much, Adam, and I want Alicia to be happy—and I know she cares a lot for you."

I put a great deal of pathos into my tone and it was most effective. Adam looked ashamed and then he reached out

71

and hugged me, the sort of painful, big-brotherly hug a man sometimes gives you merely to relieve his feelings.

And just at that moment, who should come strolling up but Brose Gilman! He often drops in unexpectedly, but he couldn't have picked a worse time. I suppose Adam was embarrassed, anyway he hastily removed his arm from about my shoulders and this made it much, much worse! Brose immediately jumped to the conclusion that that casual embrace really meant something!

I murmured weakly, "Hi, Brose—looking for me?"

And Adam stammered, "Hello, f-fella."

Brose spoke in the most utterly cold and implacable tone I have ever heard. "I can see I wasn't expected!"

I never knew he could get so mad and naturally I was tremendously flattered. But imagine my dismay and astonishment when he simply glared at me once and then, without another word, turned on his heel and stalked off.

I called pleadingly, "Brose, don't be a dope! Come back."

And Adam yelled, "Hey, listen—you've got me all wrong!"

But Brose paid no attention whatever and I was never so utterly thrilled in my life. I was sorry, too, of course, but not awfully worried, because I was practically certain Brose would forgive me.

Adam said, "That's the pay-off! Now I seem to have got you in a jam, too, kid. I'm sorry."

"That's okay," I said magnanimously. "He'll get over it." And then I was silent for a long time, thinking. When

I had things all doped out, I inquired in an enigmatic tone, "Adam, if Brose can be that jealous, how much more jealous could Alicia be over you?"

Adam, who is somewhat dumb at times, merely said, "Huh?"

So then I went into details, my idea being that if Alicia had cause to be jealous, she'd be more anxious to forgive Adam than if she was sure he was waiting around abjectly, not looking at another girl.

"But why would she be jealous?" Adam asked. "She knows I don't give a darn about any other girl."

I pointed out, "She doesn't actually have to have cause—any more than Brose had cause just then. So long as a person thinks there's something to be jealous over—" I proceeded to outline the scheme I'd figured out, which, briefly, was as follows: We'd pretend Adam had invited me to his fraternity dance in Alicia's place. She would suffer bitter pangs of jealousy. Then, too, if I knew her as well as I thought I did, she couldn't bear the idea of my being able to take her boy-friend away from her. She'd have to forgive him in self-defense. And then everyone would be happy and I could wear her second-best formal and go to the Hi-Y dance with Brose—provided Brose didn't stay mad at me.

It took me a while to persuade Adam, but at last I succeeded. When he left, I came in to tell Alicia all about our date but she had gone to bed and locked her door, so I guess she was already a little jealous over the mere fact of our sitting out in the car talking for almost an hour.

While I was getting ready for bed, it occurred to me that I hadn't written Janet a letter all week. So I sat down right then and dashed one off. It was a nice long newsy one, too. I told her Toots was fine and that he and Midge had been so good lately it was little short of miraculous. I mentioned Dad's suggesting facetiously that they must be coming down with something and Mom's saying, No, it was just her kind but firm discipline. Then I went on to tell Janet all the latest developments between Alicia and Adam and me and Brose. And I asked her whether she thought there was the slightest chance Brose would stay mad at me.

I wasn't actually worried, but a little reassurance would help. And, after all, being married, maybe Janet knows more about men than I do.

Chapter Eight

SISTERS ARE SO DIFFICULT

I got up a little late the next morning, maybe because I had stayed up so long the night before writing to Janet. Dad was just leaving for the office as I came downstairs, so I gave him my letter to mail. Then I kissed him goodbye and hurried on into the dining-room. Midge and Toots had just finished their breakfast and were scrambling down from their chairs as I came in. They trooped off to the library to play for the fifteen minutes or so before Midge was due to start to school. So that left just Mom and Alicia and me at the table, which gave me a golden opportunity to spring my news.

I said very innocently, "Mom, couldn't you possibly do something about a new formal for me? Or can I wear Alicia's as long as she isn't going to be using it? Either her new one or her black net would do."

Alicia let out a low moan like a tiger defending her young or something and said, "Mother, will you make her let me alone? She certainly can't wear my clothes."

Mom said, "Of course not, Tobey. Your yellow dress is lovely. And for a high-school club dance right here in town—"

This was the opening I had hoped for, so I said, "Oh, no, Mom, not a high-school dance. You see, Brose is mad at me and Alicia's mad at Adam, so we're going to Adam's fraternity dance together."

Alicia gasped hoarsely, "We? You mean—you and Adam?" Her voice went off into such a funny little squeak at the end, I kept my face serious by a supreme effort.

"Why, yes. Isn't that all right?"

Alicia exploded furiously, "It's just lovely! I'm so glad—for you both!" And with that she burst into tears, which she seems to do very easily, and tore away from the table and up to her room, slamming the door forcibly behind her.

"Oh, dear," Mom said. And then she regarded me very strangely. "But—Tobey, I can hardly believe this. You mean—Adam wants you to come up to college for his dance?"

I knew he didn't really want me to, but I didn't have to tell Mom a lie. I said, "After all, if Alicia chooses to pass him up, that doesn't mean he's taboo, does it?"

Mom said uncertainly, "Well—no. But it seems queer."

I finished my toast hastily and jumped up from the table before she could think of any more questions. "I have to rush now. I sort of overslept."

Mom nodded. "Hurry. Don't be late for school."

I grabbed up my books and coat and got away fast. I felt pretty complacent about the whole affair, because I could tell just by the way Alicia had taken the news that she would die before she would let me go anywhere with Adam. So it seemed as though everything was under control.

Brose ignored me all day at school, but he looked definitely unhappy, so I didn't worry. I felt pretty sure I could get around him when the time came.

I really thought, though, that he'd hold out longer than he did. My power over him must have been stronger than I'd realized. Shortly after dinner that night our doorbell rang and when I went to answer it, there was Brose. My heart leaped at the sight of him, standing there looking sheepish and apologetic. I knew we were going to make up and I was glad.

"H'lo, Tobey."

"H'lo, Brose."

"I—" he gulped, and his face got sort of red, "I wanta talk to you."

I nodded and led the way into the library where we could be alone. There was a fire in the fireplace and the lamps cast a sort of rosy romantic glow over everything and it was a very fitting place indeed to make up a quarrel. I saw now why Alicia and Adam liked this room so well.

When we were seated, Brose said in a sort of strangled

voice, "Gee, Tobey—will you—that is—you see, I got pretty sore last night, seeing that wolf, Adam, with his arm around you and—and—"

At this point there was a slight sound behind us and I looked around and saw with horror that Alicia had followed us into the room. She was standing just inside the doorway with what I can only describe as a ghoulish expression on her face.

A sense of the most awful foreboding filled me.

Alicia drawled in a positively poisonous tone, "Oh, but Brose, you don't understand. Tobey is Adam's latest conquest. He's taking her to his fraternity dance Saturday night and everything."

I could see Brose stiffen and I tried to think of something to say that would let him know it was just a ruse. But what could I say without enlightening Alicia, too?

Before I had anything figured out, Brose demanded, "But what about the Hi-Y dance?"

Naturally I floundered, with Alicia standing there gloating. "W-well, you see, Brose—I can explain if only—"

Brose shook his head and fixed me with a cold unwavering stare. "You needn't explain a thing. Just answer me. Do you have a date Saturday night with Adam?"

I gulped miserably, "Well, yes—but, you see—"

Brose said frigidly, "That's all I want to know! I've been wishing I'd invited Mary Andrews—now I can do it."

With that he turned and left and I could have died.

The front door slammed after him. I said chokingly to Alicia, "I hope you're happy now!"

She answered calmly, "At least I'm happier than I've been for some time!"

I suddenly couldn't stand any more, but I managed to leave the library with dignity. And I didn't cry until I was upstairs in my own room with the door shut. Even then I didn't cry very long—tears are so futile. I lay there on my bed, staring up at the ceiling, trying to figure things out—only they wouldn't figure.

After a while I heard the doorbell ring again and I jumped up and sneaked out to the head of the stairs to see if it was Brose. But it wasn't. It was Adam that Alicia was letting in and he must have driven down from college again just to see her. I could tell by the quavery way Alicia said, "Hello, Adam," that she meant to make up with him. And then they went into the library and shut the door.

Well, that settled things.

I went numbly back to my room and undressed and got into bed, even if it was only eight o'clock. What did I have to stay up for? It is hard to understand how a person can get into such a dreadful jam when his motives are as admirable as mine were. After all, one of my main objectives had been to get Alicia and Adam to make up. Well, now they were making up, but nothing had worked out as I intended, simply nothing at all. Brose was still furious at me and he would take Mary Andrews, who is *not* one of my favorite people, to the Hi-Y dance. And when Alicia and Adam got through in the library, he would be all set to take her to his fraternity dance and I would be left out in the cold.

My last waking thought was that it was a good thing I hadn't got a new dress because under the circumstances it would only be wasted . . .

I was quiet and sad the next morning at breakfast and Alicia was positively glowing. But no one seemed to notice either of us. Midge and Toots behaved like two little fiends, upsetting milk, arguing and crying, almost coming to blows. They kept both my parents busy trying to maintain some semblance of order and when they had finally left the table, Dad inquired with heavy sarcasm, "What happened to your kind but firm discipline this morning, my dear? A few more such meals and I'll have ulcers."

"You'll have them?" Mom sighed. "What about me?"

"We'll have them together," Dad conceded. And he added plaintively as he retired behind the financial page of the morning paper, "We're getting too old for this sort of thing."

"Adam and I," Alicia announced beatifically, "have made up. So I'll be going up to college tomorrow for the week-end after all."

"How nice," Mom said. Then she frowned at me as a thought occurred to her. "But—yesterday morning you told me you were going with him, Tobey."

"I changed my mind," I said quickly. After all, a girl has her pride. I only hoped Adam hadn't spilled the whole scheme to Alicia in his zeal to make up. And apparently he hadn't, or she would have begun gloating over my discomfiture then and there.

Instead she said merely, "Or he changed his mind," in a slightly snippy tone. And then she fingered his fraternity pin, which she was wearing on her sweater again, and smiled a knowing superior smile, as much as to say that surely no one could take Adam's interest in me seriously.

I finished my breakfast in dignified silence and left for school.

Every time I encountered Brose in the hall, we ignored each other pointedly. And once when I saw him he was deep in conversation with Mary Andrews and didn't notice me at all.

I walked part way home that afternoon with Barbie Walters. Barbie has dark hair cut in bangs and is cute and wears harlequin glasses with red frames. We have been best girl friends ever since we were in fourth grade. All my innermost secrets are safe with Barbie and vice versa. So naturally, when she inquired why I was acting lower than an angleworm's tummy, I told her all the details. I thought maybe it would help a little, just getting it off my chest.

When I had finished, Barbie sympathetically offered me half of the candy bar she had in her pocket and which she had evidently intended saving till after our paths separated. She exclaimed, "How absolutely ghoulish of Alicia!"

I nodded, chewing the candy without really tasting it.

"And of Brose," Barbie added. "He should have had

more confidence in you than that. And to take Mary Andrews, of all people! She makes me tired, she and her airs, just because she imagines she's a glamour girl!"

I sighed. Barbie meant well, but talking about it didn't help. "It's just one of those situations a person has to bear alone," I said. "But I am never going to forgive Brose Gilman for the way he has treated me—never as long as I live."

"Well," Barbie said through a mouthful of chocolate and peanuts, "I guess I wouldn't either. Men are such dopes—all but a few of them, that is."

I knew she was thinking of Sox Trevor. I didn't feel it would be fair to disillusion her by pointing out that they were all alike, really. But she'd find out, just as I had . . .

I dragged through the rest of the day and woke up Saturday morning determined to keep so busy I wouldn't have time to think. My mother was pleasantly surprised when I cleaned up my room without her even having to suggest it and ran the vacuum around the living-room and dining-room and library as well. Midge and Toots were still acting as though they had a grudge against the world and getting in each other's hair every other minute, so all of us had our hands fairly full with them.

Alicia was catching a one o'clock train and Dad had intended to drive her to the station. But when the time came, he had the children so contentedly playing with Toots's electric train that Mom suggested he keep on amusing them and let me drive Alicia to the station. I didn't mind. Anything to keep busy and keep my mind off my troubles was my idea. But I do think Alicia felt a little uncomfortable and ashamed of having messed up my date, especially since everything had turned out so well for her.

At the station as she got out of the car, she said, "I'm sorry you won't be going to your dance, too, tonight, Tobey. Really I am."

"Well," I said dully, "you have fun, anyway."

Alicia nodded. I can't remember ever having seen her in such a mellow mood. She said, "If you were going to the Hi-Y dance, I wouldn't mind if you wanted to wear my black net."

"Thanks," I said, trying to smile. "Only I'm not going."

I sat in the car and waited till the train had pulled out. I was just going to start the motor, when who should walk past but Brose Gilman and he looked as though he had suffered. He stared straight at me and my lip sort of trembled, although I was too proud to speak first, after all that had happened between us, including Mary Andrews. And so Brose went on and my heart fell, but then all of a sudden he turned around and came back with a determined stride. He yanked open the door of the car and climbed in beside me.

And then he said, indicating the departing train, "I expected you to go on that, not Alicia."

"Was that why you came down to the station?" I inquired.

Brose glared at me. "How come you decided not to go

with the mildew after all?"

"He and Alicia made up."

Brose's voice sounded sort of hesitant. "That—was pretty hard on you, I suppose?"

"Don't be sil!" I answered hotly, stung by the utter absurdity of the idea that I cared a darn what Adam Wentworth did. "You know what I think of Adam— I've told you often enough. This whole set-up between us was merely a ruse to make Alicia jealous, so she'd stop being so goofy."

"A ruse?" Brose seemed to be sitting somewhat closer to me, although I hadn't noticed him move. "You mean you actually weren't planning to go to the dance with Adam after all?"

It took quite awhile, but we got all the details straightened out eventually.

Finally Brose laughed and said, "Well, I hope you didn't take me too seriously, either—all that stuff I spouted about asking Mary to the Hi-Y dance. I guess I just wanted to hurt you, Tobey."

I inquired in a hushed tone, "Didn't you ask her?"

"That hag?" Brose said. "Of course not. I figured I'd go stag if I went at all—but now, if it isn't too late, Tobey . . ."

So we went to the dance and had a simply terrif time! Alicia's black net looked too utterly divine on me and Brose sent me a lovely spray of gardenias to wear with it. I guess there is really no other man in the world quite so wonderful as he.

SISTERS ARE SO DIFFICULT

Imagine my astonishment on waking up Sunday morning to learn the reason why Midge and Toots had been such unutterable little blights lately. Mom got worried over their symptoms last night and had the doctor come and take a look at them. So I sat right down and spent the greater part of the afternoon writing a nice long newsy letter to Janet. I not only told her about her child, but I threw in all the exciting details about the dance and about Alicia and Adam and Brose and me. Because, after all, she's probably going to need a little cheering up when she learns that Midge and Toots are both in quarantine with chicken pox.

Chapter Nine

ALICIA MEETS A DRAGON

Chicken pox in the house isn't nearly so much of a nuisance as I imagined it would be. For one thing, all of us grownups had had it, so we weren't affected by the quarantine. And, for another, neither Toots nor Midge was very ill. They looked awful, all covered with little red bumps, but they didn't feel bad, except for the itching. And the worst of that was over in a few days. So then it was merely a matter of waiting for the rash to disappear and keeping Toots and Midge amused in the house. Things got a bit hectic at times, but within about three weeks it was all over.

The dark cloud had a silver lining to this extent. My mother, who is always trying to, lost five pounds. And she didn't even have to diet. She got a simply super new gabardine suit to celebrate. So Dad said that in the long run it was the man who paid, just as it always was. But he didn't really seem to mind.

Dad was away on one of his business trips for a couple of weeks in February. Mom hates to have him gone and things sort of deteriorated around home, especially the meals. That's to be expected in a household composed entirely of women, except for Toots, of course, who is really too young to count as a male. It wasn't long after Dad's return that we got an ecstatic wire from Janet, saying that Jimmy had finally wangled a transfer to California and that they'd be home almost at once to pick up Toots.

Before we had had time to get used to the idea of not having him around anymore, Janet and Jimmy had come and gone, taking their offspring with them. They were only in Edgewood a few days, as Jimmy had to report for work at once and they were both anxious to get settled in their new home. It was really cute the way Mom worried over whether Janet would take proper care of Toots and gave her all kinds of detailed instructions, just as Janet had given Mom before. Women are funny, especially mothers and grandmothers.

You have no idea how much we missed Toots, although it was certainly a lot more peaceful with him gone. Talk about the calm after the storm! The only way a person could enjoy calm and quiet around a block-buster like Toots was to wear earmuffs and blinders. And the fact that we really felt lost with him gone only goes to prove you can get used to anything.

Even Brose remarked that it seemed kind of queer without Toots around and that he actually missed the sound of his childish screams while playing Cops-and-Robbers with Midge. I am so glad Brose is fond of children. Personally, I intend to have four—of assorted sexes, however. And while I haven't decided for sure that Brose is going to be their father, still I think a man is sort of cold and unnatural who doesn't like children.

Spring wasn't very nice this year, cool and rainy. But along toward Easter it improved a little. During spring vacation the weather was mild enough for our crowd to have a bicycle hike and weenie roast out in the country and that was lots of fun. Nothing tastes so good as half-raw weenies, burned crisp on the outside in an open fire, after a couple of miles of bike riding.

Adam Wentworth was home from college the week after Easter. Naturally Alicia was very happy to have him around and, for a wonder, they didn't have a single serious quarrel. I have never known two people who could fight so wholeheartedly and with so little reason, and then make up with such enthusiasm. It is really sort of thrilling to watch, like a fireworks display or something.

But during the week in early April while Adam was home, they simply billed and cooed all the time. And the upshot was that they decided to get married in June. No one was particularly surprised about this. After all, they've been engaged several months, so it seemed to me high time they got around to getting married. I for one do not believe in long engagements. When I make up my mind to marry a man, I am going to marry him, although I haven't any intention of reaching such an important decision for some time yet. Even if I do start wearing Brose Gilman's class ring when he gets it, that doesn't constitute an actual engagement, but is more a pledge of lasting esteem and warm friendship. This is clearly understood between Brose and me, as we have had several serious discussions on the subject since he first broached the idea New Year's.

But, to get back to Adam and Alicia, there was really nothing to keep them from getting married whenever they wanted to. Although Adam still had a couple of years to go before he would be a full-fledged doctor, money wasn't any obstacle. His father might be a little tight in some ways, but he heartily approved of early marriage and he liked Alicia very much, so he was delighted to hear they had set the date for their wedding. He immediately offered to increase Adam's allowance handsomely and promised them a Caribbean cruise for their honeymoon as a token of his complete approval.

My parents offered no objection, either, as they were fond of Adam and knew that he and my sister were very much in love. Mom didn't think that two months left quite enough time to get ready for such a momentous event, but she said she'd do her best. Dad thought this was ridiculous. He said women didn't manage their time properly and that he'd be willing to bet that he could make all arrangements for any wedding, no matter how elaborate, in two weeks, let alone two months. My mother merely smiled. Then, abruptly, her smile faded.

She asked anxiously, her glance on Alicia and Adam, "But—where will you live? A college town's bound to be dreadfully crowded. Have you thought about that?"

Alicia beamed proudly at Adam. "It's all arranged. Adam's thought of everything, haven't you, darling?"

Adam grinned, "Well, I thought about that anyway."

He went on to explain that he had tentatively reserved one of the Quonset huts that flanked the University campus. He finished, chuckling, "I had my mind made up I was going to put on a high-pressure campaign this week to talk Alicia into a June wedding. So I rented the Quonset with my fingers crossed, hoping I could persuade her."

Mom looked a little doubtful. "A Quonset hut?" she repeated faintly.

"Now, Laura," Dad admonished her. "Don't be old-fashioned. Ever so many marriages are starting out in Quonsets these days and going very well, too. In our day a three-room apartment was the absolute minimum for a young couple. Who knows, by the time Midge grows up, maybe a telephone booth will suffice."

"Oh, they're darling, Mom, really," Alicia assured her. "When I went up for Adam's dance in January, we had lunch with Jane and Joe Davis, who live in one of them. Joe's awfully tall and he has to sort of hunch down in some parts of theirs, but I don't really think Adam will have too much trouble."

"Well," Mom said doubtfully, "I suppose it'll be all

right, if it's the way other young couples are living. But it seems so gypsy-ish . . ."

On Sunday afternoon, the last day of spring vacation, an event of what seemed to be world-shaking importance took place. This was a formal call, by Alicia and Adam and his father, on Adam's great-aunt, Miss Tess Wentworth.

I couldn't blame Alicia for feeling pretty jittery over the whole business. Everyone in Edgewood knew of Miss Tess Wentworth, but very few knew her personally. Her house, a great gingerbready affair with a three-story turret and an enormous bay window bordered in stained glass, was one of the town's oldest landmarks. It was set far back behind a tall fence, with, actually, an iron deer on the lawn and a hitching post at the curb. There were heavy old-fashioned lace curtains at the windows, so that you couldn't see in. And Miss Tess herself scarcely ever went anywhere, so you never saw her. It was said she occasionally walked in her garden in mild weather, but since this was behind the house and completely surrounded by high hedges, no one caught so much as a glimpse of her. But Mr. Wentworth and Adam frequently called on her and treated her with such respect that Alicia said it amounted almost to worship. So naturally, nothing would do but that Aunt Tess must meet Adam's intended bride.

Alicia did her hair over three times and changed her dress at least twice getting ready. She was in quite a state.

"Now, dear, just relax," Mom told her soothingly, as

we both hovered around trying to be helpful. "You look very nice. Doesn't she look nice, Tobey?"

"Super," I agreed. "Aunt Tess'll love you."

"I look awful," Alicia moaned. "But Adam said dress conservatively. Do you think I look conservative enough, Mom? That awful old woman!"

"Now, dear, there is absolutely nothing to work yourself into such a state over."

"But why don't Adam and his father come?" Alicia wailed, hurrying over to the window and peering out. "It must be nearly three and that's when we're due there. Adam warns me not to be late—"

"They're not late," Mom reminded gently. "It's only a little after two-thirty. They'll be here soon. And I know you're going to have a lovely time."

"I won't," Alicia denied, brushing at a purely imaginary speck of dust on her skirt. "I'll spill my tea. I'll knock something over. Adam says her house is full of absolutely priceless antiques and that means a lot of bric-a-brac."

"All right," Mom said in a calm tone. "Is that anything to get so excited over?"

"After all the briefing Adam's given me, I know it's going to be the most ghastly afternoon I've ever spent. I'm sure of it!"

None of us had realized Midge was hanging around unobtrusively, till she said in a solemn tone, "The kids at school say she's queer. Aren't you scared?"

"Hush, Midge," Mom admonished her. "That isn't

a nice way to talk. Miss Wentworth is very old, maybe a little eccentric."

"That's the same as queer, isn't it?" Midge insisted.

Mom gave her a warning look. She told Alicia, "Everything will go off beautifully, I'm sure. If you'll just relax, dear. Stop twisting your gloves."

Fortunately the Wentworth's car drew up outside just then and Adam rushed in to get Alicia. "Thank goodness, you're ready," he said, as she came down the stairs with Mom and Midge and me at her heels. "My father didn't think he'd better come in, for fear we'd be delayed. We don't want to keep Aunt Tess waiting."

"*I*," Alicia said with emphasis, "have been ready for fifteen minutes. Where have you been, may I ask?"

We didn't hear Adam's answer, as he was hurrying her down the front steps by that time. Alicia looked as though she were pulling back just a little, out of sheer contrariness. Mom breathed a sigh of what sounded like relief as the car door slammed. I couldn't say I blamed her. I felt a little relieved myself.

Dad's voice drifted out to us from the library. "What is a nine letter word meaning 'profuse'?"

"Do you mean," gasped my mother, "you've been doing a crossword puzzle during all this?"

"All what?" asked Dad in mild surprise.

Aren't men wonderful?

Naturally Mom and Midge and I couldn't wait till Alicia got home to hear all the details. Adam had to leave for college almost immediately after their return, so we weren't kept in suspense too long. As soon as the door closed after him, we started firing questions at Alicia.

It seemed the ordeal had been, if possible, even worse than she had expected. Miss Tess, she said, was tall and grim, with white hair done in the fashion of the Gay Nineties. Her black taffeta dress touched the floor and rustled when she moved and stood out as if she must have had half a dozen petticoats beneath. She wore a gold watch on a fleur-de-lis pin set with diamonds on her bosom.

"But that wasn't the worst of it," Alicia said darkly. "It was her manner that got me."

"You mean she was rude to you?" Mom asked.

"Oh, she was polite enough, like a queen being gracious to her subjects. I suppose it's partly the way she lives, all by herself in that big old house in absolutely solitary splendor, waited on hand and foot by a couple of faithful old servants who look as though they're about ready to fall apart. And then the attitude Adam and his father take toward her, they simply bow down to her. And everyone tries to shield her from even the slightest indication that the world might have changed a little during the past fifty years."

"But she's so old, dear," my mother objected. "You have to make allowances for her age."

"So she's old," Alicia agreed huffily. "Does that mean she should be encouraged to live in the past, never stepping foot out of her own grounds, summoning the people she wants to see to come to her, like Queen Victoria or somebody? The way Adam and his father act, I felt as though I ought to kiss her hand, or knock my forehead on the floor—"

"Now you're exaggerating," Mom said.

"Not very much," Alicia sniffed. "The thing is, she's so accustomed to having her every wish taken as a command that she simply orders everybody around in the most dictatorial manner. And the queer part is, they all obey her. Why, Mr. Wentworth was absolutely meek and obedient in her presence and you know how he usually blusters. As for Adam, he practically jumped through hoops! But he needn't expect me to treat Miss Tess Wentworth as though she's the dowager queen, or something. I won't stand for it!"

"Now, dear," Mom soothed her. "You probably won't have to see her more than a couple of times a year. And surely you can be gracious to her that often, for Adam's sake."

"Well," Alicia said grumpily, "not any oftener. And if Adam hadn't had to dash right off, I'd have told him so, too. It's ridiculous!"

I, for one, was glad Adam had had to dash. Otherwise, he and Alicia would probably have spoiled their wonderful record of going for seven whole days without a single disagreement.

Chapter Ten

WEDDING PLANS

*P*retty soon I began to see what Mom had meant when she said two months didn't leave much time to get ready for the wedding. I had no idea there were so many details involved. Of course, Alicia wanted a big, beautiful church ceremony with all the trimmings. I didn't blame her for that. After all, a girl's wedding day is something special and not to be dismissed lightly. I have always felt my sister Janet made a big mistake letting Jimmy talk her into simply driving over to the county seat and getting married one Saturday afternoon and then coming home and telling the family about it. True, neither of them wanted to go through all the fuss of a big wedding, still it seemed to me Janet got a little cheated. Of course, it all comes to the same thing in the end, but the trimmings are awfully thrilling and exciting.

The way Alicia went on, you'd think nobody ever thought of such a thing as getting married before. I think weddings are wonderful, too, but there's no need to get into such a complete dither as Alicia did. And my mother, who is usually a fairly calm person, was almost as bad. All during April and May, our house fairly seethed with activity connected with the wedding. And as the time shrank to weeks instead of months, the pace grew more hectic.

Mom had all the mundane details to take care of, naturally, such as what to serve at the wedding breakfast and which cateress to hire and whether old Dr. Cartwright who had christened Alicia, but was now retired, would be hurt if she asked young Dr. Beecher, whom Alicia liked better, to officiate at the wedding. Alicia concentrated her attention on things like choosing her attendants and deciding what they'd wear and selecting her wedding dress and trousseau. Then there were fittings, which took up a good deal of her time and made her nervous and irritable. Between her and Mom and their endless discussions of this and that, they got the whole family dizzy. Midge and I, as well as my father, tried to be helpful in every way we could, such as running errands and giving our opinion when requested on color schemes and the selection of flowers for the altar. Also we were patient and for the most part uncomplaining about eating canned beans for dinner on those days when Mom had been too busy to prepare anything else.

One night as we sat at the table over dessert, which

had turned out to be canned fruit and bakery cookies, Dad said plaintively out of a clear sky, "I'll be glad when the darned wedding's over."

All of us stared at him, astonished. Alicia's lip began to tremble in an ominous sort of way.

Mom said, "Why, Henry! What a dreadful thing to say!"

Dad said stubbornly, "It's true. Not that I'll be glad to get rid of Alicia. But all this fuss and upheaval—it's barbaric. The whole idea of big weddings is a survival from the dark ages."

Midge gasped, appalled, "I think big weddings are super!"

I nodded in agreement, "So do I."

"But look at your mother, worn to a frazzle," Dad argued. "Look at Alicia, nervous as a cat. I said it before and I'll say it again, I'll be glad when the whole business is over and things settle down to normal!"

Alicia burst into tears.

"Now look what you've done," Mom said severely. "Aren't you ashamed, Henry?"

Dad looked from one of us to another, all the way round the table, for any indication of support in the stand he had taken. When he saw none, he sighed. Then he said, "Not ashamed, Laura, merely outnumbered. I'm sorry, Alicia. I apologize. Now stop crying."

I felt a little like a traitor for not backing Dad up. I knew exactly how he felt. Except for one thing, I'd have wished the wedding was over, too. It was the thought of my own thrilling part in the proceedings that had upheld me during the whole mad whirl of preparation.

I was to be one of Alicia's bridesmaids. And I had never been a bridesmaid before. My dress was the most heavenly shade of aqua, nice with my coppery hair and brown eyes. And I and the other three bridesmaids were going to wear velvet headbands to match our dresses and carry the most adorable old-fashioned bouquets with paper lace frills. Oh, it would be swoony and all my friends were simply green with envy.

And I knew Midge felt exactly the same as I did. Because she was to be a flower girl and wear her very first long dress. And her hair would be all in curls and she would carry a little basket of rosebuds. This would be quite a departure for Midge, who is definitely on the tomboy side, with braids and freckles and, usually, a smudge of jelly on her chin from always eating peanut-butter-and-jelly sandwiches. I knew she was simply thrilled silly at the prospect.

So no wonder we couldn't sympathize with Dad in his subversive attitude.

One afternoon a few weeks before the wedding, Midge and I happened to be alone in the living-room. It was the first week in June. School had let out the week before and summer seemed to stretch ahead as if it would last forever. I always have a lovely feeling the first week or so after school closes, as though I'll never have to go back. I wanted to look pale and fragile for the wedding, but after that I intended to get a terrific sun-tan, playing tennis and badminton and getting in a lot of swimming up at the lake where we always spend our vacation. Summer is so wonderful.

This afternoon I was browsing through a movie magazine and Midge was eating. She practically always eats.

Suddenly she said, over and around a large bite of apple, "Tobey, I get so excited just thinking about the wedding I could bust!"

I grinned at her. Midge is nine now and doesn't seem nearly so much of a baby as she used to. "I'm sort of thrilled about it myself," I had to admit.

I stared dreamily off into space, imagining the effect on Brose when he saw me walking demurely up the aisle in that lovely dress. The Gilmans are old friends of my family, so naturally they had been invited to the wedding. But I doubted whether Brose would even notice the bride.

Midge bit into her apple with repulsive sound effects, shattering my pleasant daydream.

"Do you have to eat all the time?" I demanded. "What will you do during the wedding, sneak a snack in among your rosebuds in case you feel hungry?"

My sarcasm was wasted. Midge didn't even hear me. She was staring into space as dreamily as I had been a minute before.

She said raptly, "If anything happens so I don't get to wear that dress and be in the wedding, I'll die."

"What would happen?" I asked. "You've had mumps and measles and chicken pox."

"Oh, not to me," Midge said solemnly. "I'm taking

good care of myself. I even stopped riding my bike no hands till after the wedding in case I might break a leg or something. It's Alicia I'm worried about—and Adam."

I had a perfectly clear notion what she was getting at, but I didn't like to admit it even to myself, much less put it into words. But Midge had no such inhibitions.

She sat scowling at her apple core. "It's three weeks till the wedding. But Adam gets home from college the middle of next week. That'll give 'em a good ten days of seeing each other every day, before they get married."

She certainly had it all figured out mathematically. I waited for her to go on.

Midge transferred her scowl from her apple core to me. "And you know perfectly well, Tobey, they've never gone for ten whole days in their lives without having a terrific fight—not when he was home from college, that is."

I had to admit that what she said was true. "But they always make up eventually," I reminded her. "And they're certainly crazy about each other, or they wouldn't be planning to get married."

"They're cert'nly crazy, period," Midge said callously. She sighed deeply. "All I hope is, they don't get into any arguments before the wedding."

"Let the honeymoon take care of itself, is that it?" I kept my tone light with an effort. I was a little worried, too.

"Oh, the honeymoon," Midge moved her shoulders up and down. "They'll be married then. I will have already worn my dress and been a flower girl."

"Aren't you being a little selfish?"

Midge shrugged again. "I don't see why. They want to get married, don't they? Well, I want to wear my long dress. Anyway," she went on philosophically, "married people never seem to have as many things to fight about as single ones. Look how well Mom and Dad get along. And Janet and Jimmy. Alicia and Adam will, too, I'll bet."

It was kind of cute the way she had things all doped out. I said, "Guess we just better keep our fingers crossed, Midge."

"Let's make a pact, Tobey." Midge leaned forward solemnly, her elbows on her knees. She is at the age where making pacts appeals to her imagination. "Let's make a pact that we'll do everything in our power to see that they don't get into a fight before the wedding."

"Sure," I said, "sure. Now let me finish this story . . ."

The day Adam got home from college, Alicia was feeling a bit low. A letter had just come from Janet, explaining that they couldn't get back for the wedding. It seemed she was going to have a little brother or sister for Toots around the first of the year and wasn't feeling very well. And her doctor absolutely forbade such a long trip. Naturally we were all thrilled over this news, but sorry because they couldn't be with us. Even their lovely gift of sterling silver hadn't helped much to dissipate Alicia's disappointment.

But Adam's arrival cheered her up. And she proceeded to show him all the wedding gifts that had accumulated.

Mom had set aside the sun-room for the presents, which were all stream-lined and adaptable to small-scale house-keeping, since everyone had heard how the newlyweds were going to live at first. A lot of relatives had sent checks, figuring that would make it simpler for Alicia and Adam to get just what they wanted and needed.

Now they picked their way through the stacks of beautiful loot, exclaiming in wonder and delight over everyone's generosity. They were so happy over being together again, it was sort of sweet to see them. The light in his dark eyes when he looked down at Alicia even made my heart beat faster.

When my sister showed him the checks, Adam exclaimed, grinning, "Holy sox, we're rich, baby! Is there one from Aunt Tess?"

Alicia shook her head. "No, there isn't. Nor any gift, either."

Midge and I, who had been hovering unobtrusively in the background, exchanged secret, faintly apprehensive glances. We knew what a touchy subject Adam's Aunt Tess was with Alicia. Too bad she had to come up so soon.

But it seemed our fears were unfounded. Adam merely bent down and kissed Alicia on the end of her nose. He said, "Oh, well, she'll come through handsomely when she gets around to it. Love me?"

"Oh, darling," Alicia answered warmly, "you know I do."

Both of them had apparently forgotten that Midge and I were there. So we took advantage of their absorption in each other to fade away quietly. It seemed quite safe to leave them alone together. I doubted that even Adam's Aunt Tess could provoke them to argument right now.

Things went as smoothly as could be expected the next few days. Alicia was endlessly busy with fittings and showers and Adam was busy with all the things bride-grooms have to do before they get married. They went to parties practically every night. Being a bridesmaid, I got invited to some of the parties, too, even though their crowd was a little old for me. It was sort of thrilling, although the men weren't nearly as good dancers as the boys I usually go around with. And some of their lines were awfully corny, too.

Brose got pretty mad about my being busy so much of the time and didn't hesitate to say so.

He complained, over chocolate malteds at Joe's Grill one afternoon, "It's getting so you don't even have time for a date anymore, Tobey. I have to catch you on the fly, like today."

It was true we had run into each other accidentally outside of Wentworth's Store, where I had gone on an errand for Alicia.

I looked down at the package on my lap guiltily. "She'll be fit to be tied if I don't get home pretty soon with this ribbon. You have no idea how easily Alicia flies off the handle these days, Brose. Weddings are so hard on women."

"Don't go trying to change the subject." Brose sounded positively dour. "I just happened to pass your house last night and I saw you getting into a convertible with Bill Sinclair. He's old enough to be your father."

"He's twenty-five," I corrected patiently.

"And you're sixteen."

"You'll know I'll be seventeen next month!"

"That's next month. Anyway, that Sinclair's a wolf. It sticks out all over him."

"He's a perfect gentleman, I assure you. Anyway, it was a party for all the bridesmaids and ushers he was taking me to. Nothing personal whatever."

Brose looked a little mollified. "Well, see you keep it that way, will you?"

It was so perfectly wonderful and exciting having him jealous. I felt all stirred up inside. I forgot all about Alicia and her ribbon and we sat there and had a long thrilling talk and another chocolate malted apiece. And was Alicia ever sore when I got home!

One day about a week before the wedding, Alicia called me into her room. She was standing in front of her long mirror, all dressed up, hat, heels, white gloves, everything. The contrast with my rolled up blue jeans and T-shirt was terrific.

"What gives?" I demanded. "Where you going?"

"To tea with Adam's precious Aunt Tess—again!" Alicia said with ominous emphasis. "As if I haven't enough to do without taking time out for that! Am I absolutely perfect in every detail?"

"You look swell," I told her. "But—do you have to go?"

"Oh, yes," Alicia said tartly. "She issued a summons. Naturally Adam wants me to look my best."

"Maybe it won't be so bad this time," I suggested.

"Why not?" Alicia snapped. "So long as the entire Wentworth family treat her like the dowager queen, naturally she'll walk all over them. It's ridiculous!"

Adam honked out in front just then and Alicia marched off to join him, a decidedly nasty gleam in her eye. If I hadn't had a tennis date with Brose that afternoon, I'd have worried myself silly before Alicia and Adam got home.

Adam stayed at our house for dinner that night, which seemed a good sign. At least, he and Alicia were still on speaking terms, which was almost more than I'd dared expect.

I was appalled when Mom inquired how tea had gone. Didn't she realize it was best to let sleeping dogs lie?

"Fine," Adam answered. He beamed at Alicia approvingly. "Aunt Tess likes you. I can tell."

"Can you?" Alicia asked a shade coolly. "I thought she merely tolerated me because I'm going to be one of the family."

Mom looked as though she were sorry she had brought up the subject. Dad, manlike, went on calmly eating, unaware that there was likely to be an explosion any minute. Midge flashed me an apprehensive look and I noticed that she was eating with her fingers crossed.

"Oh, no," Adam said to Alicia, a faint note of reproval

in his tone. "You just don't know how to take Aunt Tess."

"I don't see why you take her so seriously," Alicia snapped. "Would the heavens fall if she didn't like me?"

"I didn't mean it that way," Adam apologized and I breathed a little more easily. "It's just that she's so old and sort of set in her ideas. She hardly ever sees anyone but her own contemporaries, so it's hard for her to realize that girls dress differently nowadays."

"Why didn't you tell me?" Alicia asked with ominous sweetness. "I'd have worn a hoopskirt."

At that moment Midge very awkwardly upset her glass of milk, creating, to say the least, a diversion. By the time we'd got the mess mopped up and Midge had apologized for her clumsiness and told us all how sorry she was, everyone had forgotten what we'd been talking about when the accident happened. I might have thought it was an accident, if Midge hadn't taken advantage of the first opportunity to give me a secret wink.

But all her efforts proved to be wasted. A few days later, with the ceremony looming a scant twenty-four hours off, Miss Tess Wentworth's wedding gift arrived. And it was definitely the straw that finished off the camel.

Chapter Eleven

THE WEDDING IS OFF

*W*e had just finished an early dinner, Mom and Dad, Alicia and Midge and I, when our doorbell rang. It proved to be two delivery men, carrying a crate all of six feet long and a couple of feet wide and thick. The crate was addressed to Alicia and the sender was Miss Tess Wentworth. I felt a smothery sense of foreboding settle over me as Mom directed the men to take it into the sun-room.

As soon as they had gone, Dad got busy with a hammer. Alicia and Mom and Midge and I stood around in an expectant circle. My father isn't too adept with tools, so he made quite an undertaking of opening the big box, pinching his finger a couple of times and swearing mildly. But eventually the last board was loosened and Miss Tess' gift was stripped of its shrouding of excelsior. Then we all gave a sort of concerted gasp.

It was, of all things, a grandfather clock. The tallest, the oldest, the most ornately carved I had ever seen. Anything more incongruous and utterly unadapted to life in a Quonset hut couldn't be imagined.

I was afraid to look at Alicia. I think we all were. So we just stood there stupidly, staring at the grandfather clock instead.

It was Midge who finally spoke. "It's—big, isn't it?"

"Big!" the word exploded from Alicia like a cork out of a champagne bottle. "Big! Why, it's—"

"Now, dear," Mom began pleadingly, but Alicia was not to be stopped.

She exclaimed furiously, "It's the most absolutely ridiculous thing I ever saw! That awful woman! If this is her idea of a joke—"

Midge put in doubtfully, "Maybe she didn't understand that you were going to live in a Quonset."

"She did!" Alicia snapped. "I told her the last time I was there. And she nodded and smiled and said, 'How nice,' in that rasping, superior way of hers."

"Maybe she figured you could use it later on." This was my mother in her most placating tone.

"I have no intention of using it at all," Alicia said positively. "Adam will simply have to explain to her how unsuitable it is and ask her to kindly take it back. I'm going to call him up this minute and tell him so!"

With that she turned and stalked haughtily from the room, with all of us calling remonstrations after her. She shut the door hard, making it clear that she wanted her conversation with Adam to be absolutely private. The rest of us stood there staring at each other for a long minute. Then my father started to laugh and before long we had all followed suit and were indulging in what I suppose you could call a mass form of hysterics. Because there was certainly nothing really funny about the situation. It was just that the mental picture of that great carved clock in a Quonset hut was so absurd.

Midge recovered first. She broke off in the middle of a giggle and gave me a stricken look as the full enormity of the situation occurred to her.

"Why are we laughing?" she demanded. "This is terrible!"

"I know," Mom agreed, wiping tears of laughter from her eyes. "But it's so fantastic!"

"The old girl must be nuts," Dad said, between chuckles.

Midge gave me a pleading look. "Tobey, what'll we do? They'll have a fight for sure."

Only the tense of her final statement was wrong. They were already having a fight. Even through the closed door we could hear Alicia yelling at Adam. And, apparently, he was yelling right back.

We heard Alicia say furiously, "You're nothing but a door-mat where your aunt's concerned! You're afraid of her! And if you think for a minute I'd go ahead and marry you, now that I know what a coward you are—No! . . . *No!* I never want to see you again as long as I live!"

With that she hung up so hard it's a wonder she didn't break the telephone and then she burst into tears and ran up to her room. Midge was wringing her hands and I felt like it. Mom and Dad stared at each other fearfully.

"She can't mean it," Mom said, her tone low and appalled.

Dad ran his hands upward through his hair in a frantic gesture. "Women!" he said scathingly. But that wasn't particularly constructive.

"When she's had time to calm down a little, I'll talk to her," Mom said. "She can't do this!"

Dad stuck out his jaw, but he really didn't look terribly fierce. "And if you can't make her listen to reason, *I'll* talk to her!"

After a short strategic wait, they both tried, first Mom and then Dad and then the two of them together. I guess they used every argument they could think of to make Alicia change her mind. But it was no use, simply no use at all. Knowing my sister, I had been sure, just from the way she banged up that telephone, that she was in no mood to be reasoned with. The wedding was definitely off.

"But what can we do?" my mother wailed a little later, when she and Dad had drifted down to the living-room and slumped in weary dejection on the couch.

Midge and I shook our heads disconsolately, having nothing helpful to offer.

"I don't know," Dad said.

He chewed savagely on his after-dinner cigar, which had gone out long since. It seemed incredible that the late afternoon sun should still be streaming in through the west windows. I felt as though enough hours had elasped since dinner to make it midnight.

"All those people invited," Mom babbled. "All those gifts. Dr. Beecher canceled an out-of-town trip in order to be here. And we know they love each other—they'll be sorry later on. If only they weren't both so stubborn."

Or if only Miss Tess hadn't sent her silly gift till after the wedding, I thought. If only Alicia had even the teeniest smidgin of a sense of humor. If only Adam were more masterful and could boss her around and make her like it.

But there was no use indulging in wishful thinking. Midge and I stared at each other hopelessly. When I thought of my lovely wasted bridesmaid's dress, I felt sick. And I knew Midge was thinking of her dress, too, because she looked as sick as I felt. It was awful . . .

The rest of that evening passed like a nightmare. Mom went to bed with one of her migraine headaches—and who could blame her? She and Dad had decided to let things go till morning and see whether by some miracle Alicia and Adam would make up. If not—but I wouldn't even let myself think about the mess we'd all be in then. Calling off a wedding at the last minute is no simple matter. All evening I sat around hoping Adam would phone or come over. But the only time the phone rang it was Brose. And I was quite short with him, because I kept thinking maybe Adam was trying to call Alicia and getting the busy signal.

I don't suppose any of us slept much that night. I know

I didn't. And I could hear Midge doing a regular whirling dervish routine in her room next to mine. We both dragged down to breakfast late the next morning, looking wan and hollow-eyed and feeling terrible. Mom was still in bed with her headache and all the shades drawn. Dad was nowhere around. I had no idea where he'd gone.

I told Midge so when she asked me. And then I added, "Unless maybe he's gone down to notify the newspaper the wedding's been called off."

"Oh, Tobey, don't say that!" Midge sighed, dripping cereal down the front of her T-shirt and not caring. She had made me do her hair up in curlers the night before, just in case, and she was still wearing the metal clamps. They gave her a strange unfamiliar appearance. She turned her lackadaisical glance toward the window. "Why does it have to be a lovely day?"

I hadn't noticed the weather till then. Sure enough, the sun was shining. Somehow that made things seem even worse.

I quoted wryly, " 'Happy the bride the sun shines on' —only there isn't going to be any bride."

Midge eyed me accusingly. "Aren't you going to *do* anything?"

"Such as what?"

"Well—I don't know. But we made a pact, remember?"

"Then how about you doing something?" She looked so woebegone when I snapped at her that I relented and gave her hand a little squeeze. "Never mind, baby. You can be flower girl at my wedding."

"But that'll be years," Midge moaned. "Maybe never."

I was too sunk even to resent the insult.

Just then, who should wander into the breakfast-room but the cause of all our troubles. Alicia had on her old flowered chintz housecoat that faded in the wash and her hair tied up in a bandanna. She looked pale and her eyes were still a little pink from all the crying she'd done last night. But the set of her mouth was grimly stubborn.

"I just want a cup of coffee," she murmured. "My head's simply splitting and I thought maybe that would help."

"Oh, Alicia," Midge clasped her hands on the edge of the table in a beseeching gesture, "please make up with Adam and get married."

"I don't care to discuss it," Alicia said. She looked from Midge to me. "Well, don't sit there staring at me like a pair of dying calves! I guess my future happiness means nothing whatever to you, if you want me to entrust it to a man like Adam."

"But you can't have stopped loving him," I began, "just because his aunt—"

"Don't bring that woman into the conversation," Alicia cut in sharply. "I prefer to forget her very existence."

She poured herself a cup of coffee, took a few sips. "Besides, I haven't noticed Adam making any effort to persuade me to make up." She fixed Midge and me with an accusing glance, as though it was our fault. Her voice had thickened a little as she added, "It's perfectly obvious his aunt means more to him than I do—" she broke off with a sort of muffled sob, put her cup down hastily and rushed back upstairs, her housecoat billowing out behind her.

Midge emitted a miserable, "Gosh!"

We went through the motions of finishing our breakfast. Then Midge said, "Guess I'll go outside for a while," and wandered off.

I carried our dishes out to the kitchen. It was better to have something to do than to sit around brooding. I might even wash the dishes, I thought glumly. But as I set them on the sink, I thought of what Alicia had said about Adam not making any effort to persuade her to forgive him. And suddenly an idea burst into full flower in my brain. A really super-dooper idea! I couldn't imagine why it hadn't occurred to me sooner.

I went quietly out into the hall and picked up the phone and carried it into the coat closet with me. This is possible to do by stretching the cord out to its very fullest extent. Then I shut the door as tight as possible and gave the operator Adam's number. When I heard his voice at the other end of the wire, I said, very softly and persuasively, "You know who this is, don't you?"

He didn't doubt for a minute it was Alicia. People are always telling us we sound alike, especially on the phone. And this was once it was going to come in handy.

"Darling!" he exclaimed in such a husky, emotion-packed tone that I immediately began to feel terribly guilty over my impersonation. "I've been hoping and praying you'd call. You can't imagine how—"

"Adam, wait," I broke in desperately, my conscience hurting so I couldn't have stood it if I didn't feel I was doing both him and Alicia a kindness. "I think we should talk things over face to face, not on the phone."

"So do I," Adam agreed warmly. "I'll be right over, sweetheart. I know we can straighten everything out."

After we'd hung up, I hurried up to Alicia's room. She was slumped disconsolately on the chaise longue, still in her old faded housecoat, brooding. I saw I was going to have to work fast. It wouldn't take Adam more than ten or fifteen minutes to get from his house to ours, especially in his present state of mind.

"You know," I said thoughtfully, "I shouldn't be surprised if Adam came over to see you this morning."

"Wouldn't you, Tobey?" Alicia's tone sounded wistful. But then her chin grew stubborn and a gleam I didn't like came into her eye. "I doubt it. He's too contrary. He wouldn't make the first move."

"Still," I argued, "a man's wedding is pretty important to him."

"Not if he no longer loves the girl he was planning to marry," Alicia sniffed.

I shrugged. Long years of association with Alicia have taught me the best way to handle her. I knew the wisest course was to act as though what she did made no difference whatever to me.

"Even so," I said casually, "I'd get some clothes on, if I were you. I don't suppose you'd care to have him catch

116

you looking like that, if by some chance he did come over."

I went out then. But I listened from the hall for a couple of minutes and pretty soon I could hear her moving about and the squeak of the closet door opening, so I judged she was taking my advice. I went on downstairs and hovered expectantly in the hall. Only a few minutes later a car stopped on the drive and I heard Adam taking the front steps two at a time. I hurried to the door and opened it.

"Why, Adam!" I tried hard to sound and look surprised.

"Hi, Tobey," he dismissed me casually. "Where's Alicia?"

"Why don't you wait in the library?" I suggested. "I'll tell her your here."

This was truly a master stroke on my part. I know so well that the library is their favorite room in the whole house.

Alicia came out of her room just as I reached the head of the stairs after seeing Adam politely into the library. She looked very pretty in a yellow dirndl and a white peasant blouse that left her shoulders bare for her hair to curl softly against. "Tobey," she asked, her eyes shining, "didn't someone just come in?"

"It's Adam," I whispered. "What did I tell you? He's in the library waiting for you."

She went down the stairs very slowly, so as not to appear too anxious, I suppose. I followed at a discreet distance and, when she had gone into the library and shut the door behind her, I sneaked up fast and locked it. Because, naturally, I was afraid of what might happen when she found out that Adam hadn't come entirely of his own accord. And if they quarrelled again—and weren't able to get out of the library!—I was practically sure they'd go ahead and make up. If those two were shut up together anywhere for ten minutes, they'd get into each other's arms. So I was the gal who was going to see to it that they stayed shut up together long enough for nature to take its course. A nice warm glow of achievement settled over me as I pulled the key quietly out of the lock and dropped it into my pocket.

I sat down on the bottom step of the stairs, not to listen, just to wait. I could hear the sound of voices faintly from the library and in a very short while they grew louder and more emphatic, as though Alicia and Adam were starting to argue. Then I heard high heels tap angrily over to the door. The knob turned and rattled and Alicia's voice called sharply, "Tobey! Tobey!"

I sat quiet like a mouse. Soon she gave up calling and jiggling the doorknob. I heard Adam's voice, then hers, then his again. Even without being able to distinguish any words, I could tell their tones were growing less angry by the second. Before long they were talking so sweet and low I couldn't hear anything but a gentle murmur, with long, expressive silences in between. I had just about decided it would be safe to release them and fade out of the picture, when to my astonishment the front door opened and my father and Adam's father sailed into the hall.

I simply sat there, staring up at them blankly.

"Where is Adam?" Mr. Wentworth demanded, scowling down at me. "We went home first to look for him and the housekeeper said he was here. Of all the fool nonsense, quarreling with Alicia on the eve of their wedding and not even telling me about it!"

"Can you imagine," Dad put in, "Jeff didn't have any idea what had happened. He was completely in the dark."

"If you hadn't come down to the store and explained the situation," Mr. Wentworth beamed at my father, very man-to-man, I probably wouldn't have known a thing about it until it was too late. Now we're going to get this mix-up straightened out in short order."

"Shhhh," I admonished, eyeing the library door anxiously. "I think they've got it straightened out themselves, if only you two—"

I broke off incredulously, staring past Mr. Wentworth and my father. The front door had opened once more and through it Midge was triumphantly piloting a very old, very grim-looking lady in black taffeta that rustled and a hat like a velvet pancake bristling with ostrich plumes.

Mr. Wentworth whirled around at the sound of that rustle, his gaze following mine. "Aunt Tess!" he exclaimed blankly.

"Where," Miss Tess Wentworth demanded in the rasping voice Alicia had described so accurately, "is Adam? Why didn't the young scamp explain to me what a Quonset hut was? How was I to know a grandfather clock wouldn't fit in? Nobody tells me anything! If it weren't for this sweet child—" she laid a black gloved hand on Midge's shoulder and smiled down at her affectionately, blue jeans, soiled T-shirt, hair-curlers and all, "I might have been the innocent cause of breaking up a lovely romance."

"But, Aunt Tess," Mr. Wentworth gasped, rushing to slip a solicitous hand under her elbow as though he were afraid she might collapse any moment, "how did you get here—who told you—why—"

"Don't sputter, Jefferson," Miss Tess squelched him. "This child has more sense than any of the rest of you. She came to me and explained everything, thank goodness. Naturally, I didn't want to waste any time about setting things straight, so we came in a cab."

"A cab?" Mr. Wentworth squeaked in horror.

My father put his hand hastily over his mouth and I knew that he was smiling behind it. The Edgewood Cab Company has "Speed and Safety" for its slogan, but the accent seems to be on speed. I had a hard time to refrain from bursting into laughter at the mental picture of Miss Tess streaking through the streets at breakneck speed, after scarcely setting foot outside her own grounds for some twenty years. But she seemed none the worse for her experience.

She announced, beaming, "Of course, I'll take the clock back and keep it till Alicia and Adam get a real home. In the meantime, I'll give them a check, so they can buy something they can use right away."

Just then I became abruptly aware that Alicia was

again jiggling the doorknob and that she and Adam were demanding in unison to be let out and to know who was out there.

Everyone looked a little blank as I fitted the key into the lock and turned it. All but Midge that is. She and I gave each other a knowing wink. When we two make a pact, we really keep it . . .

Chapter Twelve

WEDDINGS ARE WONDERFUL

*F*or a wedding day that had begun as such a complete mess, I must say that Alicia's and Adam's wound up most satisfactorily. Mr. Wentworth proceeded to take Aunt Tess home with the utmost care and caution, so that she might rest from her unheard of exertions until time for the ceremony. Mom's headache got better quickly, once the cause of her nervousness and tension had been relieved. She and Alicia flung themselves into the last minute preparations with fine fervor, with Dad and Midge and me helping in every way we could. I did manage to get Midge alone long enough to demand a few details as to just how she had succeeded in getting Miss Tess to accompany her to our house.

"It wasn't hard," Midge denied. "She's not a bad old lady when you get to know her. I was a little scared just at first, but as soon as I made myself march into that spooky old house and talk to her, I knew there wasn't anything to be afraid of."

"But what did you say? How did you tell her about Alicia getting mad at Adam on account of her wedding present without hurting her feelings?"

"I was awful tackful," Midge admitted with no false modesty. "But I just told her the truth. And as soon as I realized she didn't have any notion what a Quonset was like, I saw how it would be easy enough for her to make a mistake like sending that big clock. So I explained things politely and she understood right away. And when I told her there prob'ly wasn't even going to be any wedding and about my beautiful dress and the rosebuds and all, she said we must waste no time straightening things out with Alicia. The cab was my idea," she added, "but Miss Tess didn't mind at all. I kind of think she got a kick out of it, once we were started."

Midge was interested to know how I'd happened to lock Alicia and Adam up in the library, so I explained all about that. What with one thing and another, time passed very quickly and almost before we realized it, the hour had come to get ready for the wedding.

I don't think I have ever spent a more thrilling and exciting day. My dress was just beautiful and so was Midge's and everything went off with such wonderful smoothness it seemed almost incredible. As I walked slowly down the chapel aisle to the stirring strains of the wedding march, all the turmoil and confusion that had gone before seemed like a fevered dream. Midge looked sweet and demure with her little flat basket of rosebuds and her long pale yellow dress. Alicia made a lovely bride. And even Adam, except for looking a little green around the gills as men always seem to at their weddings, made a very satisfactory and handsome bridegroom.

I stole a quick look through my eyelashes as I passed the pew where the Gilmans were seated. Brose was staring straight at me in absolutely entranced admiration. Needless to say, my heart swelled and I was glad I had gone to all that trouble to bring Alicia's wedding off as scheduled. With Brose's eyes devouring me as though I were a piece of wedding cake, it all seemed terribly worthwhile.

Of course, I had a pretty strong hunch Midge felt she deserved most of the credit for bringing Alicia and Adam back together. And Dad looked just a little smug as he led the bride up the aisle to the flower-decked altar, so I wouldn't be surprised if he felt it was really his conference with Mr. Wentworth that had turned the trick. Oh, well, I thought as the minister's voice began to speak slowly and thrillingly, we all deserved some credit. Team-work was the important thing and we had certainly had that.

Later, when the reception at our house was under way and I had a little free time, I told Brose all about it. I knew I could rely on his not letting the story go any further and I felt as though, if I didn't get to tell someone, I'd pop.

"You mean," Brose demanded, his eyes all bugged out with astonishment, "the wedding came that close to falling through?"

I nodded. Brose and I were sitting in our usual spot on the hall stairs, since all the downstairs rooms were simply swarming with wedding guests. Brose was holding one of my hands and playing with my fingers, bending them gently back and forth as he seems to like to do. I don't mind it, either.

He said, "Holy cow! I never knew any other family that seems to have as many crises as yours does. How do you stand it?"

I said, "Well, at least life is never dull around here."

"Golly, no," Brose agreed. He bent my fingers back and forth some more, then curled them up in a little tight ball and closed his hand around them. "Look, Tobey, how much bigger my hand is than yours."

I couldn't see anything so surprising about that. "Look how much bigger you are than me." Brose is nearly six feet tall and still growing.

"Yeah, I know—but—gee, you've got a cute little hand, Tobey." He frowned. "Gee, I'll bet you're going to swim in my class-ring, though. How will you keep it on?"

That was easy. Ever so many girls I knew had the same problem. "You wind the inner part of it with thread, silly. Unless—" I couldn't resist teasing him just a little, "unless you'd rather I didn't wear it."

Brose stared at me, appalled. "Oh, no! Golly, no,

125

Tobey. I can't *wait* to have you wear it. The jeweler's promised to have our rings ready in October. I'm counting on you wearing it then."

I relented. "Okay. I will—unless we don't feel the same about each other by that time."

"Why do you always talk like that, Tobey? I know I'll feel the same about you."

"I'm pretty sure I will, too, Brose. But—we're sort of young. And people change."

"We won't," Brose said positively. "I won't let us." He held my hand tighter. "Gee, though, when I saw you walking up the aisle in that long dress, sort of as though you were floating—" His tone grew very solemn. "Tobey, if we do decide to get really engaged when we're older—and then married later on—promise me you'll wear a dress just like this one for our wedding."

I thought that was terribly sweet of him. "But brides usually wear white," I reminded. "White, with a train. And a veil, like Alicia wore."

"I don't care what color it is," Brose said sort of hoarsely. But—long and—soft and—beautiful, like this dress." He smoothed a fold of it gently with his palm.

"Okay." My voice was a little husky, too. "I promise."

My mother spoke so unexpectedly from just above us on the stairs that we both started and Brose dropped my hand guiltily. I had forgotten she was up there, helping Alicia change and get ready to leave, until she said quietly, "Tobey, Alicia wants to see you for a moment before she goes. Can you come now?"

Of course, I jumped up and followed her to Alicia's room. Mom didn't come in, but closed the door quietly after me.

Alicia looked breathtakingly lovely in her beige suit, with the smart black accessories that set it off so perfectly. She seemed different, somehow—more poised and sure of herself, warmer and gentler. But marriage—just an hour or so of marriage—couldn't really have changed her. I must be imagining it.

She stood there, with her back toward the mirror, smiling at me. Her new beige luggage was packed and ready near the door. Already her room looked different, so neat and impersonal, somehow. The realization struck me that it wasn't going to be Alicia's room anymore and I felt queer.

"Come here, Tobey," Alicia said.

I guess I looked pretty solemn as I walked across the room toward her. She asked, "What's the matter?"

"N-nothing," I gulped, "only—I just suddenly realized that you aren't going to live here anymore, Alicia. I—knew it, of course. But I didn't think till this minute what it'll mean."

Alicia's smile widened a little, but it wasn't an objectionable sort of smile—I mean, she seemed so gentle and understanding, she wasn't like the same person. She said calmly, "Well, it's nice to think you'll miss me, Tobey. But after we get back from our cruise, I won't be very far away, you know. Just living with Adam's father the rest of the summer and then up at college."

"But you won't be *here* in this house—you won't ever live here again—and coming back for visits won't be the same."

"You're sweet, Tobey." Alicia's arm went around my shoulders. "And don't think I don't appreciate what you did for me this morning."

She knew then that the library door getting itself locked hadn't been any accident as I had implied. And probably Adam had told her about the phone call, which he had thought was made by her. And she was thanking me—Alicia was thanking me. Marriage certainly had changed her, even in a couple of hours!

She went on, "I've already thanked Dad and Midge for helping, too. You were all so swell. And I realize now I was very foolish, acting as I did. Now that Adam and I are married—" her voice softened, just saying his name, "well, I realize how dreadful it would have been if I'd let anything spoil things."

"Gee, Alicia—gee—" it seemed to be all I could say.

She gave me a little hug and pushed me toward the door. "You'll know what I mean someday, Tobey—when you're in love—and just married. Now run along, like a dear. And tell Adam I'm ready."

The next few minutes were wonderful and thrilling. I got hold of Adam and he went upstairs for Alicia's bags. As the two of them came down together, Adam carrying the suitcases and Alicia close behind him, all the guests congregated in the hall to see them off. They went out the door in a perfect snowstorm of confetti and good wishes and ran down the steps to Adam's car, that was parked on the drive. Someone had put an enormous JUST MARRIED sign on the back and tied a bunch of cans and a cow-bell and some old shoes to the rear bumper.

When I was younger, I used to get a kick out of doing things like that—now it seemed very childish and silly. I had a hunch some of Midge's cronies had fixed up the car, but maybe not. Some grown-ups have perfectly infantile senses of humor, so you never can tell.

As the car drove off, the last I saw of Alicia was her gloved hand waving out the window. It made me feel almost like crying, although I can't imagine why. My mother was crying, just a little, and Dad was patting her shoulder and saying soothingly, "There, now, Laura . . . don't, honey . . ." and things like that.

Everyone began talking and laughing and drifting back into the house. But I still felt funny and sort of choky. And then someone pressed a large clean white handkerchief into my hand and I blew my nose hard and felt better. Of course, it was Brose and he is really wonderful and so understanding, just like my father. We walked over to the end of the porch and I sat down on the railing and Brose stood close beside me and patted my shoulder.

He said, "Why do women always cry at weddings? Don't you think Alicia and Adam will be happy?"

"Well, of course," I said. "It isn't that."

"Then what is it?"

"Well, it's just," I had to sort of grope to find the words I wanted, "it's just that marriage is such a big, important step—and for their whole lives and all—it—it sort of scares you. That's why we cry—only I didn't really."

"I don't know," Brose teased. "My handkerchief feels pretty wet."

I grinned up at him. "To tell you the truth, this is the very first wedding I ever went to when I felt like—even a teeny bit like crying. Maybe that means I'm growing up."

"Maybe."

"For that matter," I said with a little giggle, "this is the first wedding I ever went to when I didn't have a finger in decorating the bridegroom's car."

"Is that so?" Brose said, so casually that I knew darned well he'd had something to do with tying all that junk on Adam's car.

I guess what they say is true, about women maturing much earlier than men. But I decided not to say anything about it to Brose, especially when everything was in such a nice dreamy state betwen us. Instead, I said, "Just think of that heavenly honeymoon cruise Mr. Wentworth is giving them. Isn't it swoony to think of being on a big luxury liner, nosing its way lazily through the azure waters of the Caribbean, with a tropic moon rising majestically over the palms of a romantic island?"

"Sounds like you've been reading too many travel ads."

"Oh—you!"

"Take it easy," Brose laughed. "I was only kidding. Sure it would be swell to take a cruise like that—with you. Only I doubt whether my dad could afford to give us one. He has a heck of a time just paying his income tax."

Men are *so* unromantic.

"Anyway," Brose went on softly, picking up my hand, "I think it'll be swoony this summer just going up to Green Lake like we always do. I don't need the Caribbean, so long as we can take a nice long canoe ride, just the two of us, and watch the moon rise over Gull Island."

Maybe they aren't so unromantic, after all.

I said dreamily, "Remember the beach picnics we've had, and the driftwood fires?"

Brose nodded. "And the way the moon makes a path across the water, so wide and yellow it looks as though you could walk on it?"

"And the way music sounds on a portable phonograph, outdoors that way and sort of drifting off into nothingness?"

"And the way hot dogs taste, with the outsides all crisp and maybe a little sandy and the insides raw?"

We looked at each other and I knew Brose was thinking of exactly the same thing I was. I said, "Stop, you're making me hungry!"

"Making myself hungry, too."

It was swell to think of summer looming ahead and all the wonderful times we'd have, just as we had other summers. But in the meantime—"Come on around to the kitchen," I said in a very confidential whisper. "I'm pretty sure there's some ice cream left in the freezer, maybe even some chicken salad."

Brose grinned at me and we ran down the steps hand in hand and around the corner of the house toward the kitchen.

Chapter Thirteen

THE SOUTHERN MENACE

*N*aturally, our family suffered a sort of let-down after Alicia's marriage. Things were bound to seem a little dull after all that excitement and upheaval. But it was a rather nice sort of dullness. A bit of calm and quiet around the Heydon household would certainly be something in the nature of a novelty. Compared with last winter, when Janet and Toots had been staying with us, and we had all sort of milled around and got under each other's feet, our house seemed practically empty with only four people living in it. We almost rattled around.

Of course, there were advantages and I'd be the last one to deny them. I never had to wait for the shower anymore. No one ever borrowed my best nylons without asking—and snagged a run in them! When the phone rang, it was practically always for me. And Brose and I could play all his Harry James records any time he cared to bring them over, without Alicia breaking in and wanting to play something drooling by Sinatra, just because she was lonesome for Adam and wanted everyone else to suffer, too.

With the wedding out of the way, I got seriously to work on my tanning, so that I'd have a good head start before we went up to Green Lake. We always go to our cottage there for the month of July, as that is when my father always takes his vacation. Green Lake isn't swanky or anything, but it is a pleasant place and has the added advantage of only being about seventy-five miles from Edgewood. Ever so many people we know have cottages there, including the Gilmans and Barbie Walter's family. So it is always fun and we all look forward to July. Mom always gets a grand rest, which she said she could certainly use after all the energy she had expended getting Alicia married. Dad wears his oldest clothes and doesn't shave any oftener than Mom makes him. And he goes fishing every single day, which is his idea of Heaven— although frankly, we all get a bit fed up eating the results of his hobby. And I mean that literally! Midge has a lot of friends at the lake and she practically lives in the water, or scrabbling about in the sand. And as for me, well, there are just so many things I love to do at Green Lake that I couldn't begin to list them. The Gilmans' cottage is next door to ours and they always come up in July, too. So Brose and I have a simply super time—at least, we always have had a simply super time.

How was I to know this summer was going to be so perfectly awful?

For one thing, our vacation plans were thrown out of gear at the start by Dad's having to make an unexpected business trip east the last week in June. He thought he'd be home by the first of July, but he proved wrong. The rest of us would have gone to Green Lake without him and let him join us there, except for the fact that Mom developed some trouble with a wisdom tooth and had to stay in Edgewood to have it treated by the dentist. So what with one thing and another it was the eighth of July before Dad got home, Mom's tooth was better and we were off in a cloud of dust for Green Lake. The Gilmans had gone the first of the month as we had all planned to and I can tell you those eight days of waiting for everything to shape up were hard on Midge and me. We moped around like nothing human, feeling sorry for ourselves and getting in each other's hair generally. When we finally locked up the house and started off, our car loaded down with the usual assortment of summer paraphernalia, I heaved a blissful sigh, figuring all my troubles were over. That was what I thought!

Fool that I was, I couldn't wait to see Brose. And, naturally, I supposed he was feeling the same about me. Later I was to realize it was those eight days that did it— caused all the trouble, I mean. The person who dreamed up that adage about absence making the heart grow fonder certainly didn't expect the absentee in question to be exposed to the potent influence of a girl like Kentucky Jackson. But I was serenely unaware of the existence of Kentucky that lovely July morning when we arrived at Green Lake.

I didn't even think much of it when Brose didn't come over right away. It always takes hours and hours to clean up the cottage after it's been closed up for the winter. And since Brose must have gone through all that when the Gilmans first came to the lake, it seemed perfectly reasonable to me that he wouldn't want to get embroiled in another clean-up job. We all pitched in, Mom and Dad and Midge and I, sweeping and scrubbing, brushing down cobwebs, making beds and generally getting the place presentable.

Every year Mom wails, along toward the middle of the cleaning job, "I don't know why I go through this! It's ridiculous! Why don't we simply sell the cottage and stay home? We have a nice comfortable house in Edgewood, but do we have the sense to stay in it?"

Dad says, "I couldn't fish in Edgewood."

Midge says, "I couldn't swim."

I add, "Or go canoeing."

We all sound so wistful that Mom admits grumpily, "Oh, well—I enjoy the lake, too, once this—this mess is over."

So then we all fall to heartily once more and get the mess cleaned up. This year was no exception but along toward late afternoon we had the cottage in good shape and I decided to go for a swim to cool off. Midge had sneaked off a half an hour or so before. Mom and Dad were too exhausted to think of swimming. Dad was too exhausted to even think of fishing, before the next morning, that is. So I knew he was really tired.

I got into my new two-piece yellow bathing suit, grabbed up my bathing cap and started out. Mom and Dad were sprawled comfortably in deck chairs on the screened porch, drinking iced tea and looking as though they might fall asleep any minute.

Dad gave me a look of paternal appraisal through half-shut lids and murmured drowsily, "Have fun, Tobey, but don't get wet."

Dad's humor is so corny, but he means well. I smiled at him sweetly and went on.

Naturally, I detoured past the Gilmans' cottage to see Brose. I was beginning to feel just a little slighted. It seemed at though he might have risked coming over before this, even if he did hate housework and fear he might be roped into helping with some of our cleaning. Still I didn't really hold it against him. So I went up the Gilmans' path and stood on their top step to peer in through the screen door. Mr. and Mrs. Gilman were sitting exactly as my parents had been, only the pitcher on the table between them held lemonade instead of iced tea and they had already dozed off. It seemed a shame to disturb them, since obviously Brose was nowhere around. Evidently he had already gone down to the beach. So I considerately descended the steps on tip-toe and went on along the path that led to the lake.

Kicking up the warm loose dust with my bare feet, enjoying the sunshine, the thought occurred to me that it was sort of odd Brose hadn't stopped by for me. But I didn't really have a premonition that something was wrong. I told myself maybe he hadn't got my card telling the date of our arrival, maybe he hadn't noticed the signs of activity next door. The lake cottages are fairly far apart, so this seemed perfectly probable.

I strolled cheerfully along, sniffing the nice wet familiar smell of the lake ahead. It was an indescribable smell, but I loved it and my pace quickened a little. Then across a stretch of yellow sand, I glimpsed good old Green Lake itself, just as always. The little waves nibbled at the beach as though they liked the taste of it. A mile off shore the dark green of Gull Island looked like a big blob of spinach. A bunch of little kids, very shrill and skinny, were splashing in the shallow water. I was sure Midge was among them. Farther out, around the white painted diving raft, a dozen or so friends of mine were swimming. They were mostly girls, as seems usually to be the case at summer resorts. There wasn't a sign of Brose anywhere.

Where was the big lug, I wondered, frowning. And then, only a few feet from where I stood, I saw him.

Back at the very edge of the beach, where scrubby bushes cast a cool border of shade, there was Brose. He was lying on his tummy, his chin in his hands, gazing up soulfully at a girl who leaned against a bright canvas backrest. And what a girl!

Her hair was pale blond, like silver-gilt, and done in a

soft long page-boy, with not a strand out of place. She was looking down at Brose, so I couldn't see the color of her eyes, but her lashes were terrific. She reminded me a little of several movie stars and none of them had a thing she didn't have and hers was displayed to super advantage in a sarong-type bathing suit with great splashy crimson poppies on a white ground. She looked as though she hadn't been any nearer the water than she was right now —and didn't intend to get any nearer. Her skin was a soft creamy white like magnolia blossoms. And the proprietary, adoring way she was smiling down at Brose made my flesh creep.

I simply stood there, staring, with my mouth open like one of Dad's freshly landed fish. Something queer and painful was happening inside me. Because it was quite obvious that Brose, who had scarcely looked at any other girl but me since we were both mere infants in Junior High, was lying there facing me, so close I could have thrown sand on him, and not seeing me at all. It made me feel like the invisible man or something! In vain I tried to reason with myself, reminding me that I was blond, too, and that nobody had ever run shrieking at the sight of me —not in the opposite direction.

But it didn't do any good. There was something sinister about that girl's absolute perfection, something that made me feel like Gravel Gertie's kid sister. And, somehow, I just couldn't bear to speak to Brose at that moment, when he was so utterly bewitched. Instead, I simply pretended I hadn't noticed him *or* the beautiful stranger.

I ran right across the beach, waving and calling gaily to my friends in the water. I splashed in, buckling my bathing cap under my chin and trying not to gasp as the cold water hit me. I didn't pause—Brose just might be looking, although I couldn't count on it. I swam out to join the others with my very best crawl.

Everyone yelled cheerful greetings as I swam into the midst of the crowd around the diving raft.

Barbie Walters hugged me and shrieked, "Tobey, we've missed you!"

Kay Lamb, another special friend of mine, seconded, "We sure have. It isn't the same without you, Tobey."

"Oh, you just say that because it's true," I cracked.

But they had made me feel a little better. Among the bunch of familiar faces clustered about, I saw Gil Forrester and Itchy Stearns, who, with Kay and Barbie and Brose and me, had formed an inseparable six-some for many summers. Sox Trevor's family doesn't come to Green Lake, so Gil Forrester has long been Barbie's summer boy friend. Now with the old summer crowd all around me, I could have been quite happy and content if it hadn't been for the nagging thought of Brose, lying up there on the beach exposed to all that glamour. Not, of course, that I let any of the gang suspect for a moment that I wasn't happy and content.

We all swam around, laughing and splashing each other and yelling friendly insults back and forth. Finally, out of breath, I pulled myself up onto the raft and lay there, feeling the sunshine settle over my wetness like a warm overcoat. I pulled off my cap and let my damp hair fall forward over my face. After a minute or two someone plopped down beside me and I turned my head on my crossed arms to look up and see who it was. Barbie Walters grinned at me.

"Hi, Tobey. Mind company?"

I shook my head.

Barbie took off her bathing cap and sat there, chewing the strap of it contemplatively. Barbie's hair looked like wet seaweed, the same as mine did, I imagined. Her tan was much deeper than mine, but then look at the start she had on me. She'd already been at the lake three weeks.

Barbie said, "I thought maybe you preferred to be alone with your sorrow."

Sometimes Barbie is almost too discerning.

"What sorrow?" I asked lightly. Or, at least, I hoped my tone sounded light.

Barbie and I were all alone on the raft at the moment. But she put her lips close to my ear in a very hush-hush manner to say, "You don't have to pretend with me, Tobey. You saw her, didn't you?"

"Who?" I asked, all innocence, although probably Barbie knew me too well to be fooled.

She did. "Don't give me that," she admonished, her tone pitying. "You couldn't practically trip over a dish like Kentucky Jackson and not see her! Not with Brose Gilman panting at her feet!"

"Oh, you mean *that* girl," I said. Then I did a sort of incredulous double take. "Did you say her name was— Kentucky?"

Barbie nodded. "Can you imagine it? Even if she is from Louisville."

"She's new, isn't she?" I asked.

"Not as new as the rest of us in one sense," Barbie said a trifle tartly. "She's twenty if she's a day, I'll bet. But she's new at the lake, if that's what you mean."

My heart sank. Where had I read that every man had to have at least one love affair with an older woman?

Barbie went on, "Unfortunately, there aren't any men her age around. So Kentucky's out for the boys in our crowd." Barbie is usually quite a tolerant person, but she sounded bitter now.

"Who is she staying with?" I asked.

"The Warrens. She's their niece and she's spending the summer here with them. So there isn't the slightest hope of getting rid of her."

"But surely," I objected, "if she's twenty, she can't be seriously interested in boys of seventeen."

"That's what you think!" Barbie said. "She's been here ever since we came to the lake three weeks ago, so I've had plenty of chance to observe her. She can be interested in anything that wears pants. She has Gil and Itchy positively drooling. And since the Gilmans came up, she's been working on Brose."

"But they say there's safety in numbers." I tried to ignore the sinking sensation in the pit of my stomach. "She can't grab off all the boys here."

"Hah!" Barbie said without humor. "Take a look back there on the beach, if you think she can't!"

I did so—and gulped. Brose was still stretched out at Kentucky Jackson's feet, but he had been joined in the last few minutes by Gil and Itchy and a couple of other boys who must have slipped unobtrusively away from the crowd around the diving raft. They were all clustered about that delectable bit of date-bait while the rest of us girls took refuge on the raft, or swam around defiantly trying not to look deserted.

I murmured weakly, "Her line must be super."

"Sugar," Barbie sniffed, "till it gags you! And all in the most terrific Southern drawl. The boys eat it up, natch."

"And that's not all." Kay Lamb clambered up on the raft beside us and jumped into the middle of the conversation with both feet. "She's a one-woman fashion show all the time. You know how it's always been at the lake, Tobey. We could sort of let down and really enjoy ourselves, live in blue jeans or bathing suits and do our hair in pigtails to keep cool. And the boys didn't care, they didn't think anything of it. But now!"

Barbie took it up, "Kentucky's got them conditioned so they expect glamour from morning till night. She actually comes to beach picnics in white sharkskin slacks!"

"And she's got *three* bathing suits," Kay exclaimed, "not that she ever goes into the water! And she wouldn't

143

dream of getting tanned—it coarsens the skin so, she says. She makes the rest of us look like a bunch of Indian squaws by comparison."

I jumped to my feet. I didn't know just what I was going to do, but it seemed to me the time had come for some sort of action. Barbie and Kay eyed me expectantly.

"Well, come on," I said. "Let's not just huddle around out here like a—an abandoned harem, or something! Let's swim back in and at least offer Kentucky a little competition."

Chapter Fourteen

THE MENACE IN ACTION

Barbie and Kay and I swam back and trudged over to the shady edge of the beach where Kentucky Jackson was holding court. It looked as though all she lacked was a crown and scepter. She was certainly surrounded by her loyal subjects.

Brose glanced up at me in astonishment. "Why, Tobey! When'd you get here?"

"Today," I told him. "Didn't you get my card?"

"Oh, is today Saturday?" he came out of his fog then sufficiently to introduce me to Kentucky Jackson.

She gave me a smile of absolutely dazzling sweetness and I saw that her eyes were a deep, soft, almost violet blue—darn it! How could anyone be so perfectly beautiful and live?

She drawled, "It's just wonderful meetin' you, Tobey,

honey. I've heard so much about you from everyone."

Her accent was really something to hear. So far as Kentucky was concerned, the letter 'r' might as well have been left out of the alphabet.

I murmured something appropriate and Barbie and Kay said hello to Kentucky, too, filling up an empty gap in the conversation.

None of the boys seemed to mind our joining them—or maybe they just didn't notice us. Even Brose's gaze wandered back to Kentucky, as though he hadn't the slightest control over it. I felt sick.

"Do sit down, darlings," she invited us graciously. "You must be simply exhausted after all that exertion." Her tone was so syrup-y you could have eaten it on pancakes.

"I'm not a bit tired, thank you," I said and stayed on my feet out of sheer defiance.

"Neither are we," Barbie and Kay echoed.

"I declare," Kentucky shook her head, so that her silver-gilt hair swung against her shoulders, "you Northern girls are so energetic, I simply marvel at your endurance."

She made us sound as though we were constructed of cast iron, or something.

"Don't you swim?" I asked.

"Oh, I know how," Kentucky drawled. "But the sun's so scorchin'." She smiled directly at me again. "Brosie's been tellin' me what old friends you two are."

Brosie—I'd heard her say it with my own ears and he

146

hadn't turned a hair. If I'd called him Brosie, he'd have tossed me into the lake.

I said, "Oh, yes, we've known each other a long while."

"You're so fortunate," Kentucky told me. "Here I've only known Brosie a little more than a week. Look at all the time I have to make up." She actually reached out and laid her hand on Brose's as she said that. And I thought for a moment he was going to purr.

How much flattery can a man stand, I wondered?

Finally I caught Brose's attention long enough to ask, "Aren't you going to swim at all?"

"Huh?" he asked blankly.

"Swim—you know?" I repeated. "In the water?"

He looked down at his bone-dry trunks and then up again a trifle sheepishly. "Oh, that's right, I haven't been in yet."

Kentucky smiled languorously at him, "It's so nice here in the shade, Brose, honey. Who wants to swim?"

I said, "It's what people usually go to the beach for."

"Not I," Kentucky said sweetly. "The water's so bad for a person's hair—makes it all stringy." Her blue glance just touched my hair.

I could have slapped her.

Brose said doubtfully, "The water looks good, though." He glanced my way. "Okay, Tobey, I'll race you to the raft."

As he got to his feet, I couldn't resist giving Kentucky a triumphant smile. But she was already starting to concentrate on Gil and Itchy, so maybe she didn't notice.

We ran splashing into the water and swam out, with Brose pulling ahead and yelling back, "Come on, slow-poke . . . Get a little steam up . . . Don't go into reverse on me," and all sorts of amiable insults like that. It would have been just like old times if it weren't for Kentucky, lying back there on the beach, waiting to pounce on him again.

He reached the raft yards ahead of me and when I swam up, he accused, "You're out of practice, hag. Want some lessons?"

"Not from any beach-hound, I don't!" I spluttered.

"Who's a beach-hound?" Brose splashed water in my face and I splashed right back at him. That relieved my feelings a little.

"I'd like to know what else you call it."

"You kids just haven't learned the art of relaxation," Brose said loftily. You kids—can you imagine? Putting himself in Kentucky Jackson's age bracket and making like the rest of us were years younger!

I glared at him. "You might try giving Kentucky swimming lessons. Maybe then she'd get her suit wet!"

"The idea's got possibilities," Brose said dreamily. "Maybe I will."

Before I could think up a cutting answer, he went on, "It's fun having someone new at the lake, don't you think? The same old crowd all the time gets a little dull."

"I do not!" I snapped. "I like the crowd just as it's always been."

"Oh, sure," Brose agreed. "I like 'em, too. We've

always had fun. But with Kentucky around, it's just that much better."

That, I thought, was strictly a matter of opinion. But I didn't say so. I hate cats. Besides, I doubt whether Brose would have heard me, even if I had spoken. He was craning his neck to see what was going on back on the beach.

"C'mon, Tobey, I'll race you in," he said abruptly. And off he swam without even waiting to see whether I was following!

Naturally, when I reached the beach again, I stalked right on across it and up the path toward home. Brose Gilman, all the rest of the boys, could spend the entire summer at Kentucky Jackson's feet, so far as I was concerned. But I'd be darned if I was going to hover around and watch!

Back at our cottage, I dressed defiantly in blue jeans and T-shirt and braided my hair in pigtails. After dinner Midge and I did the dishes, because Mom was so tired. Midge couldn't wait to get through to rush out to join her friends again. I didn't feel in any special hurry, so I did an elegant job of sink cleaning and even rinsed out the tea towels afterward. When I was finally finished I went outside and sat on the back steps awhile, watching the sunset. There was an old tennis ball lying on the ground so I got up and began bouncing it lackadaisically against the porch railing.

Pretty soon Barbie and Kay appeared. They were wearing playsuits I hadn't seen before, very pretty and new-looking. They had even managed to get their hair to curl a little bit since our swim.

"Traitors!" I said.

Kay blushed, but Barbie said firmly, "you were the one who said we ought to give her a little competition."

"I changed my mind," I explained, and bounced the tennis ball hard against the porch railing several times. "Why should I spoil my vacation copying her, dressing up like a—a store-window dummy, or something? If people don't like me the way I am, the way I've always been, they just needn't like me, that's all!"

Barbie insisted, "It won't do a bit of good to act like this, Tobey. Dress any way you please, but don't waste your time moping around alone figuring Brose will come hunting you."

Kay put in, "We both tried being stand-off-ish when Gil and Itchy first went for her, but they didn't even notice."

Barbie said wistfully, "We'd have tried to make them jealous—only there weren't enough other boys around."

The shortage of teen-age males at Green Lake is always fairly acute, but it had never bothered me before because I'd always had Brose. And men Kentucky's age are even more scarce. Apparently she already had found that out.

"What burns me up," I exploded, "is that the big dopes haven't enough sense to realize she's only using them because there aren't any older fellows available. Why, I'll bet if anyone over twenty turned up—"

Kay sighed, interrupting, "We know that. We tried

telling Gil and Itchy so, too, but they didn't believe us."

"The male ego, you know?" Barbie said sarcastically. "She has every last one of them convinced that he's the one she really likes best. Don't ask me how she does it."

"Flattery," Kay suggested. "And the way she looks at them—as though they're simply terrif. It's sickening, but all the boys love it. I don't think she could get away with it, though, without that southern accent. I mean, it would sound perfectly silly, coming from us."

"I'm not going to try to copy her," I said sharply. "As for Brose and Gil and Itchy, they can do anything they like. I don't care what they do!"

"It's what you're going to do that matters," Barbie said sensibly. "If you're smart, you'll do like Kay and me, simply make the best of things."

I asked warily, "You mean get all palsy-walsy with Kentucky?"

"Not necessarily," Kay said. "But at least be civil to her. Then the crowd can go on doing things together, hiking and playing tennis and swimming—"

"Kentucky doesn't swim," I pointed out.

"She doesn't want to do anything that would get her mussed up," Barbie agreed. "But so long as the hikes aren't too long and there's a shady spot for her to hold court in while the rest of us swim or play tennis—"

"What a dumb way to spend a vacation!" I burst out.

"Not so dumb as—for instance—bouncing tennis balls around all by yourself," Kay said pityingly.

I saw what she meant . . .

So that was the way my vacation started out—the vacation I'd looked forward to for weeks, that I'd thought was going to be just as much fun as other summers. And things didn't get any better, either. We all took little sissy hikes, with Kentucky in glamorous play clothes and Barbie and Kay and I defiant in blue jeans and sneakers. Occasionally we were able to beguile the boys into a good hot set of tennis, provided there was a shaded deck-chair nearby for Kentucky to loll in. We swam, with the boys tearing themselves away now and then from Kentucky who reclined on the beach under a sun umbrella. It was perfectly putrid!

My family didn't realize anything was wrong. Dad fished every day and sunburned his nose as usual. Midge swam and built sand castles. Mom had lots of friends at the lake, so she had fun playing bridge and swimming and reading the books she hadn't had time for all winter.

Of course, they all met Kentucky, but just seeing our crowd around together, they had no idea what a fly in the ointment that southern menace was for Kay and Barbie and me. In fact, all the older people at the lake thought her perfectly charming, including my parents. Funny, how undiscerning people get after they're forty. I hope I'll be more understanding with my children's problems, if I ever have any children. Somehow, I wasn't so sure about that as I used to be, seeing Brose and Kentucky together.

Because it soon became clear that she was concentrating most of her wiles on Brose. Oh, she was still being sickeningly sweet to any other boys who happened to wander into range. But her most enchanting smiles, her warmest looks and most honeyed accents were lavished on Brose. I couldn't imagine a thing like that—or could I? The way I felt, I didn't even trust my own judgment anymore. And I was too proud to discuss the matter, even with old friends like Kay and Barbie, so I couldn't get an unbiased outside opinion. I only suffered.

Since Kentucky slept late, I did get Brose to myself sometimes in the early morning. But even when we were alone, things weren't the way they used to be. That woman seemed to exert some sort of foul spell over him, even when she wasn't exactly around in the flesh.

One day I accused him, when we were sitting on our back steps right after breakfast, "You act like a zombie or something when Kentucky isn't around! Snap out of it, stupid!"

Brose brought his wandering attention back from some far distance. His tone was reproachful. "Why do you girls always pick on Kentucky? She thinks you're sweet kids, all of you. She often says so."

"Kids!" I exploded. "She makes us sound around six years old—and not very bright!"

Brose shook his head. "Kentucky says girls never understand her. That's why she prefers the company of men."

"Men! Does she pretend to consider you and Gil and Itchy men? Why, she's old enough to be your aunt, or something!"

Brose leaned his elbows on his knees and stared dreamily into space. "What's a year or two difference in age? Besides, I seem older—as old as the average college senior."

"She told you that, too, I suppose?"

"Why, yes, she did."

I jumped up. Suddenly I couldn't bear it, seeing Brose, of whom I am very fond, make a complete fool of himself over someone who didn't really appreciate his finer qualities at all. How can men be so blind?

I said, "If you ask me, you aren't even acting as old as a high-school senior! More like eighth grade, I'd say. You're being such a dope!"

He didn't even get mad. That sort of scared me. Didn't anything I said make the slightest difference to him anymore?

He got to his feet and stood there, regarding me with a sort of pitying condescension that made me see red. And then, as though it were the most natural thing in the world, he reached into his pocket and pulled out a *pipe*.

My mouth dropped open. "Brose! You don't smoke?"

He cradled the pipe bowl in his fingers caressingly as he shook his head. "Not yet. I promised my folks I wouldn't till I'm eighteen. But Kentucky loves to see a man with a pipe, so I just bought it to carry around, sort of get the feel of—"

I broke in, "I think that's the silliest thing I ever heard of! I think you're nuts!" And with that I turned and rushed into the house, slamming the screen door after me.

I didn't dare look back. Because I knew that if Brose was standing there, staring after me with that pipe in his hand, as if he were Ronald Colman or somebody, I'd throw something at him. Or else I'd burst into tears. And that would be worse—much worse!

Chapter Fifteen

THE BEST LAID PLANS

Even though I wasn't having much fun, time passed very quickly at Green Lake. There are always so many things to do on vacation, I suppose it's bound to seem as though there aren't enough hours in the day. Even with Kentucky Jackson casting a pall over all our crowd's activities, still we kept so busy I didn't have much opportunity to brood. Which was just as well, because it hurt me so to think about her and Brose, I don't believe I could have borne it if time had hung heavy on my hands.

When the day came for Kay and Barbie to go home, I felt pretty sunk. I'd known all along they'd be going back to Edgewood before I did, as their folks had come to the lake so much sooner than mine. Still it was hard to face their going, as we were such good friends and had sort of lent each other moral support in our troubles with Kentucky.

Kay didn't feel too badly about leaving, as Itchy Stearn's family was going at the same time and I guess she thought she could get things back on the old basis between them once he was away from Kentucky's influence. And Barbie didn't mind, either, because after all, Gil was only her summer stand-in and once she was home she'd have Sox Trevor again and Sox had never even heard of Kentucky, except as a state, which was something altogether different.

"Chin up, old girl, and all that sort of rot," Barbie counseled staunchly in farewell.

And Kay added, "At least you can be thankful Kentucky doesn't live in Edgewood. You can make Brose forget her once you get home."

Somehow their words weren't as comforting as they meant them to be. I didn't want to have to make Brose forget anybody. I didn't want him to like me best in Edgewood simply because another girl had gone back to Louisville. I remembered all the times we'd sat on the stairs at home, with Brose holding my hand and bending the fingers back and forth. Did he do that with Kentucky when I wasn't around, I wondered? My throat ached at the thought. Maybe he'd rather have Kentucky wear his class ring than me. That thought hurt even worse than the other one. If I didn't look out, I'd be bursting into tears right in front of Kay and Barbie.

I tried to smile, but it wasn't very convincing. I said,

"I guess I can stand another week of her, but it's going to be tougher without you two."

And it was.

With Barbie and Kay and Itchie gone, our crowd had shrunk to four. Just Kentucky and Brose and Gil Forrester and I were left. We still got together to do things, but I didn't feel as though anyone would have missed me if I weren't there. I was getting more and more bitter over the fact that my whole vacation had been a miserable flop and it was all Kentucky's fault. Well, it was Brose's fault, too, of course, if you wanted to look at it from an absolutely unbiased viewpoint. Still, I felt Kentucky was more to blame. You could hardly expect a boy Brose's age to hold out against her. But did she have to grab off simply every man in sight?

And then, out of my rankling resentment, an idea sprang full fledged. It was just like it had been the day I thought of locking Alicia and Adam in the library so they'd have to make up and get married. Only this time my super-dooper scheme was for my own benefit. I saw it all clearly, in every detail, the way to make Kentucky suffer a little for all the trouble she'd caused Barbie and Kay and me. It was too bad I hadn't thought of it before the others left, because I knew they'd have loved being in on it. But just because I'd have to carry it out all alone didn't bother me a bit. It was going to be fun squaring accounts with Kentucky. And she certainly had it coming . . .

I didn't breathe a word of my plan to anyone. I couldn't

risk something leaking out to make Kentucky suspicious. Besides I didn't have any really close friends around in whom to confide. Keeping it all bottled up inside made me feel sort of like a champagne bottle just before the cork pops out. But I managed to conceal my excitement.

One afternoon at the beach I suggested innocently that we hadn't had any moonlight picnics at Gull Island in quite a while.

"So we haven't," Brose agreed.

Gil piped up, "Why don't we have one tonight, just the four of us?"

And even Kentucky said it sounded like fun.

"We can take hot dogs and stuff. There's always plenty of driftwood for a fire," Brose went on.

"Sure," Gil agreed. "And maybe have a moonlight swim."

Kentucky shivered daintily. "That doesn't appeal to me, but the rest sounds wonderful. I just adore moonlight picnics."

It scared me a little, the enthusiastic way they all fell in with my suggestion. As though it were fate, or something. I said, "We could paddle out in Gil's canoe," and sort of held my breath to see whether there'd be any objection to that.

But there wasn't. They all thought that was a swell idea, too. It looked as though my scheme wasn't going to encounter a single snag. I couldn't have been happier.

We started out around eight o'clock. It was a hot, still evening, with a sort of breathlessness in the air. Or maybe that was just my own secret excitement. As Gil paddled along toward Gull Island, we all joked and laughed and sang songs. Kentucky sat just ahead of me, trailing a lily-white hand in the water. Gil and Brose and I wore jeans and T-shirts over our bathing suits. But not Kentucky—oh, no! She looked like a fashion ad in a lemon yellow slack suit and a gay printed ascot. The rest of us were bare-footed, but Kentucky wore thick-soled yellow clogs. As usual, not a curl of her silver-gilt hair was out of place. But tonight I took a sort of fiendish pleasure in her perfection.

When we were within ten yards or so of the island, I figured the time was ripe and went into sudden action.

"Look, kids!" I cried, leaping to my feet and pointing. "Isn't that a heron right over there in those trees?"

Gil's canoe lurched crazily under my tricky footwork. He grabbed for me and missed. I saw to that.

Brose yelled, "Sit down, dope!"

Kentucky just screamed.

Then—splash!—the canoe went over and we were all thrashing around in the water like crazy. I had never realized before quite how easy it is to capsize a canoe. And, I prided myself, it must have looked perfectly accidental.

As I had known, the lake was only about four feet deep at this point. I touched bottom easily and looked around. Brose and Gil were obviously touching bottom, too, but Kentucky hadn't bothered to find out how deep the water was. She had simply reached out in a panic and grabbed the nearest man—thank goodness, it was Gil!—and was hanging onto him for dear life, yelling her head off.

Gil managed to break that headlock of hers before he choked. He gasped reassuringly, "You can't drown here, Kentucky—it's all right—we can wade ashore—"

Brose began to laugh and I felt relief nibble at me. He was hanging onto the boat so it wouldn't get away. He said, "Tobey, you dope, don't you know better than to jump around in a canoe like that? But we look so darn' funny—"

"Funny!" Kentucky spluttered. The look she gave me would have shriveled anyone who wasn't too wet to shrivel. She exclaimed furiously, trying to push the plastered hair back from her face, "Of all the clumsy, stupid things I ever saw, Tobey Heydon—"

"I'm sorry," I fibbed. "I guess I just didn't think."

"Sorry!" She glared at me and opened her mouth to say more.

But Brose interrupted, "There's no use fighting about it now. Let's get ashore and make a fire and dry out our clothes."

"All the food's lost," I said, feeling a qualm of guilt. Still there was something very gratifying about the sight of Kentucky, standing there with her clothes and hair soaked, so mad she could pop.

Gil said, "Give me a hand, Brose, and we'll pull the canoe up on shore."

Suddenly a funny look came into Brose's face. He demanded, "Gil, where's the paddle?"

"Paddle?" Gil gulped, a wild gleam in his eye. "Oh,

my gosh! I had it when we started to tip—then when we went over, Kentucky grabbed me and—and I must'a dropped it—it must'a floated off—"

We all began to look around desperately, but there was no sign of the paddle.

I said, and this time I wasn't fibbing, "Golly, I am sorry! It's all my fault."

"Of course it is, you little dimwit!" Kentucky snapped. And then, managing to inject a little honey into her tone, she said, "Oh, Brosie, this is dreadful! I'm so glad you and Gil are here to take care of us."

"Sure," Brose said. "We'll take care of everybody."

We finally got a fire made, although it wasn't easy with damp matches, and we huddled around it, drying our clothes as best we could. To my utter surprise, after the first shock Kentucky cheered up, although she was still definitely cool to me. Her slacks would never look the same and her scarf had run messily, but her hair, to my astonishment and pain, proved to be naturally curly. And so, on the whole, she really managed to look better than I did.

Gil said, "Too bad we couldn't salvage those hot dogs. I'm hungry." He burped. "Sorry. I always do that when I'm hungry."

Brose said, "Better to urp a burp and bear the shame, then squelch a belch and die of pain."

Kentucky laughed as though this were the most humorous thing she had ever heard, although it was so old it had long gray whiskers. "Brosie, you're so funny."

"Isn't he, though?" I said sarcastically.

"What'sa matter, Tobey? You worried?" Brose asked.

"Of course not. Why should I be worried?" I couldn't very well admit I was feeling snappish because my lovely scheme for showing up Kentucky in a bad light seemed to have backfired.

Gil said, "When we aren't home by a reasonable hour, someone'll come out to look for us."

"Of course," Kentucky said, smiling sweetly. "It's really rather an adventure, don't you think?"

I certainly hadn't expected her to take it like that! I sat near the fire, my chin on my knees, feeling glum and empty and chilled. And then, to really top things off, it became apparent that nature was going to take a hand in the proceedings. I realized that the wind had come up and the sky was darkly overcast. Suddenly there was a long, threatening rumble of thunder. Lightning streaked down the sky and I let out a low moan. If there is anything that scares me to death it's a storm. And here I was, going to be caught out in one. It was almost like a judgment.

"Ooooh," Kentucky said, her voice all thrilled. "It's going to storm."

She actually sounded as though she were happy about it.

Gil said, "Yeah. Guess we better get back under the trees."

"Wait till it starts to rain," Kentucky breathed. "There's something so splendid about storms. I love to watch them."

Hadn't I heard somewhere that trees attracted lightning? There was another growl of thunder and a bright ominous flash. I put my face down on my knees and shut my eyes tight.

"What's wrong with her?" Kentucky sounded amused.

But suddenly someone sat down beside me and I felt an arm go comfortingly around my shoulders. I looked up and there was Brose. He was grinning down at me, but his eyes were gentle and somehow I wasn't nearly so scared. I burrowed my head against his shoulder and the thunder didn't seem so loud, nor the lightning so blinding.

"Take it easy, baby," he said, very low. "Someone'll come out for us sooner than ever if it storms. They'll figure it wouldn't be safe for us to paddle back in a canoe . . ."

Well, of course he was right. The storm had hardly got under way when my father and Mr. Warren picked us up in the Warren's motor launch. So here I am, two days later, sitting up in bed and getting over my cold and writing down all the details in my diary. And I must say, it's a drippy way to finish up a vacation. Especially since Kentucky went and told everybody that I tipped the canoe over on purpose. And even my own parents believed her and called me down something terrible.

Sometimes I wonder at the utter inconsistency of older people, especially parents! For years, all during the most formative period of our lives, they teach us to be self-reliant, to stand up for our rights and not to let our little playmates impose on us. And then, when I followed that same formula in dealing with a sugar-coated menace like Kentucky Jackson—well, you'd think I'd committed some awful offense!

And my cold's been so bad, Mom hasn't let me have any visitors, so I haven't even seen Brose. Although maybe I wouldn't have seen him anyway—maybe he doesn't want to see me, after the exhibition I made of myself that night on Gull Island.

It's funny, but just after I finished writing the above, I heard Brose calling me softly outside the window. So I put on my chintz housecoat with the yellow roses on it and a yellow ribbon around my hair and just a smidgin of powder on my nose because it is still a little pink. Then I went over to the window and Brose and I had a long talk. And he is really wonderful, probably the most wonderful and understanding man in the world.

The first thing he said was, "Tobey, I just had to see you whether you're supposed to have visitors or not. You don't think it'll make you any worse, do you?"

"Of course not, Brose," I told him. "I'm feeling much better. But you know how mothers are about colds."

"Sure, but I wouldn't want you to have a relapse. Still I just had to see you. I had to tell you I think it was very low of Kentucky to go around saying you tipped the canoe on purpose. I know it was an accident."

I felt awful, but all I could gulp was, "Do you, Brose?"

"Why, sure. And another thing," he sounded terribly in earnest. "You were right about her all along."

"I was?" I asked in surprise. "But—she was really grand that night on the island—when I went all to pieces."

"That's not what I mean," Brose said. "The thing is you were right about her just killing time with Gil and Itchy and me till someone her own age came along."

This was almost more than I'd dared hope for. I stared at Brose through the window screen and his expression was scornful. He went on, "The Warrens let her ask a friend up from Louisville. He got here the morning after the beach picnic and he's around twenty-five and none of our crowd has hardly seen Kentucky since he came. She doesn't pay the slightest attention to us."

I couldn't say 'I told you so.' I felt too sorry for Brose.

But somehow he didn't sound as disillusioned as I expected, adding, "I for one don't care what she does. I even threw away that fool pipe."

"Did you, Brose?" My heart was beating faster.

"Sure." He stared at me through the screen. "All I'm worried about is whether you'll forgive me for being such a dope. Will you forgive me, Tobey?"

After all I'd been through I should have held out a little longer. But I didn't. I murmured, "Oh, Brose, of course I will."

"Gee, Tobey, that's swell of you, after I acted like I did. I actually don't know what I saw in her. She isn't half as pretty as you—nor as sweet—"

I simply couldn't stand having him think so well of me when I didn't deserve it. I blurted out, "Brose—don't!

Kentucky was right about my tipping the canoe on purpose. It was—awful of me—but I was so mad at her, being so beautiful and perfect and all—and I just couldn't let her have you without a struggle."

I was looking down at my clasped hands, but I simply had to risk a glance at him to see how he was taking my confession. And one glance was all I needed. I knew then that it was all right, everything was all right. Brose didn't look angry at all, he looked flattered!

Chapter Sixteen

THE HEART HOP

*A*fter we got home from Green Lake the rest of the summer was lovely. The only trouble was, it went too fast, but summers are always like that, I guess. Brose's part-time job in old Mr. Haley's hardware store left plenty of time for him to do other things, besides supplying him with enough money to do them with. We saw a lot of each other, played tennis, went on bike hikes, took in a good many movies. Nothing was really changed between us, in spite of the Kentucky affair. We both agreed not to discuss that anymore, or even to think about it, and I believe that was the best course. A woman like Kentucky would be hard for any man to resist and, after all, Brose is only human. Besides, he had the good sense to get over her very fast, so it seemed the least I could do to help him forget the whole thing was let sleeping dogs lie. So I did.

Naturally Brose spent a good deal of time at our house and my father made frequent corny jokes about why didn't he just bring his trunk over and move in? But Brose is used to Dad and, goodness knows, I am. So we ignored him. My father is really very sweet and so is my mother. She always has cokes and cookies on hand for the crowd and all my friends would rather come to my house than almost anywhere else, because there's room to jitterbug and nobody minds how loud we play the phonograph, so long as we shut a few doors. I wish every girl was as lucky as I am.

Of course, nobody's life is absolutely perfect and I won't say mine is. It used to be Alicia who got in my hair. Now that she's only home for an occasional visit, we get along quite well. I think marriage has really mellowed Alicia and she is absolutely crazy about Adam, which seems to have made her disposition much better than it used to be. Now the monkey-wrench in the machinery of my life is my kid sister Midge.

Maybe something drastic happens to girls around her age, something they can't help. This would certainly be the kindest view of the matter. All I know is, my little sister had gone on for years, being no more of a blight than all little sisters are. But now, practically overnight it seemed, Midge's whole personality curdled. It became poisonality—with the accent on the poison! And as if that wasn't bad enough, she developed a terrific friend-ship with another little punk named Judy Allen. And what Midge didn't think of, Judy did, and vice versa.

The Allens had just moved to Edgewood that summer and they lived several blocks away from us, so I didn't know any of the family but Judy. She was a big-eyed little kid with almost as many freckles on her nose as Midge had, which is something of a record. Her hair was dark and she wore it in a sort of shaggy page-boy, tied back from her face with a ribbon that was usually coming untied. But it wasn't her looks I objected to, it was the absolutely devastating effect she and Midge had on each other. They were like two chemicals, harmless enough in themselves, which, added together created something only a little less deadly than TNT.

I don't know whose idea it was to experiment with my private hoard of creams and lipsticks and stuff, but both of them did it. I wasn't sure whether my dressing-table would ever look the same afterwards. They smeared my favorite nail-polish as high as their second knuckles. I'm pretty sure Midge, at least, sampled the perfume Brose gave me Christmas and which I saved for only the most special occasions. Either that or it evaporated terribly fast. But the crowning blow was the day shortly after school started in September, when I came in and actually caught Midge and Judy reading my diary!

After the calling down I gave them, I didn't think they were likely to try anything like that again. But just to be doubly sure, I began hiding the diary under my mattress. I complained to my parents, too, but I didn't get anything like proper co-operation from them.

Dad chuckled, "What you lack is perspective, Tobey."

I looked at him blankly.

Mom explained, smiling a little, "You see, dear, this isn't the first time your father and I have had to cope with this situation."

I still didn't get it. I objected, "But it's only just lately Midge has got to be such a perfect little blight."

Dad shook his head. "It's not Midge we're talking about."

And Mom added, "A few years back your older sisters found you just as annoying as you find Midge."

I answered coldly, "I was never like that—never!"

But I could see plainly neither of them believed me.

Brose proved a more sympathetic audience when I confided in him the trouble I was having with Midge.

"Sisters!" He shook his head. "They must be a pain all right."

"If you had any you'd know what a pain," I told him glumly.

It was after school and we had stopped in at Joe's Grill for malteds, as both of us were always practically starved after school and couldn't possibly get all the way home without something to eat. Brose happened to be broke, since it was the day before his allowance was due, so I was treating. I don't think things like that really make any difference where two people are such good friends as Brose and I and understand each other so completely.

Brose said, taking a deep pull on his straw, "Maybe it's just because there's so many of you. Maybe just two sisters would get along okay, but four—"

I said, "But that can't be it. There's only Midge and I left at home now and things are certainly no better. If anything they're worse. Especially since she and Judy Allen got so thick."

"You mean Judy's a bad influence?"

"Maybe it's vice versa. Anyway, they think up things together that neither of them possibly could alone."

"Such as?" Brose swished his malted round and round to get the nice gooey foam off the sides of the glass.

"Well, they actually had the nerve to read my diary once, before I found a good place to hide it."

Brose asked, his eyes sort of questioning on mine, "What sort of things does a girl write in her diary, Tobey?"

"Well," I hoped I wasn't blushing, but my face felt warm and I looked down into my malted intently, as though I expected to find a pearl or something in it, "sort of personal things. Stuff that happens and how she feels about life and people. Not anything shameful, but not the sort of thing she wants a couple of little brats like Midge and Judy to get a big kick out of."

Brose nodded his head several times up and down solemnly. "I can see how you'd feel about that. And I don't blame you a bit." He asked then, in a sort of shy way I thought very sweet, "Does it say anything about me in your diary, Tobey?"

I gave him a smile I hoped was inscrutable, like Mona Lisa's. "Maybe."

He should know how much it says about him in my diary, I thought. Why, he's practically the hero of it.

Midge seemed to grow steadily worse as time went on. I don't know which were the hardest to bear, her bratty moments or her helpful ones. She and Judy developed a burning interest in 'lovelorn' columns in the newspaper. They pored over articles on how to manage your love life and then Midge tried to give me advice. As if I needed any help in that direction!

Mom said placatingly, "If you'll just bear with her, darling, I'm sure she'll get over it. These phases pass."

"Bear with her!" I exclaimed. "Isn't it enough she and Judy stick their little freckled noses into my cosmetics and clothes and even my diary? Now do I have to stand for their advice and interference in my private affairs?"

My mother sighed. "Sometimes I think it's going to be wonderful when all of you are grown up. And then again I wonder if it won't be a little dull."

"I could stand a little dullness myself," I said.

"But, Tobey," Mom reasoned, "they haven't got into your cosmetics or read your diary lately, have they?"

"Only because I laid the law down to them—and they can't find the diary," I pointed out. "It isn't as though they'd really reformed."

One day Midge was having a light afternoon snack of chocolate cake and ripe olives and milk in the kitchen when I came in, bent on pressing my pleated skirt. I shuddered at the revolting repast spread before her and merely helped myself to an olive.

"How," I inquired with sisterly regard for what, I hoped, would someday be her waistline, "can you gorge yourself so?"

Midge said, "Hmmmm?" absently without lifting her eyes.

It was then I saw she had the evening paper on her lap, folded open at the love-advice column. This is run by a quaint character named Aunt Flora, who is nothing short of an oracle of wisdom in Midge's eyes and those of her friend, Judy, too. Seeing my sister so preoccupied, I didn't bother to repeat my remark. Instead I set up the ironing board and got busy.

Presently Midge spoke thoughtfully. "Tobey, you know what's wrong with you and Brose?"

I merely sighed and went on ironing. There is practically no use trying to stop Midge when she has just finished reading Aunt Flora. Maybe if I ignored her, though, she'd dry up.

She didn't. She went on solemnly, "You let him take you for granted, but it's a mistake not to keep a man guessing."

"No!" I said.

Sarcasm was wasted on Midge. "Yes, it is. Aunt Flora says so. Especially during the early stages of an association between a young lady and gentleman."

I pointed out, "Brose and I have known each other five years."

"Well, yes," Midge admitted, "but you're not married

174

yet, or engaged or anything. So you're still in early stages."

If I hadn't known it was next to impossible for Midge to keep a secret, I might have informed her that in just a matter of weeks, when Brose got his class ring, I would be wearing it. And even though that wasn't an engagement, it was pretty serious and important.

Instead I said merely, "Did I ask your advice, squirt? Or Aunt Flora's, either?"

After quite a long interval of silence, Midge said, "Hmmm?" again absently, so I knew she'd gone back to her reading.

That was oke with me. I finished my skirt, put the ironing stuff away and helped myself to just a smidgin of cake. I'd got as far as the hall when I remembered an important errand I had to do. Since Mom was out and someone might phone, I figured I'd better tell Midge my intentions.

"Hey, twirp," I called. "I'm going to take my coat down to the tailor's like Mom said and get it lengthened."

After awhile my sister's voice came faintly from the kitchen, "Hmmm?"

I had my coat out of the closet by that time and was on my way. "Going to the tailor's," I called back and shut the front door behind me.

I wouldn't have been away more than half an hour, if I hadn't happened to meet some girls I knew as I came out of the tailor shop. We decided to have sundaes as we were all simply starving. Isn't it ironic to think how one thing in life hinges on another? It's sort of like a game I used to play with cards when I was little. I'd stand a whole deck up two by two, in little tents in a long line across the floor. Then I'd touch the first one and they would all fall down in succession. Life is much the same. If it hadn't been for those sundaes, I'd have got home before Brose phoned and none of the subsequent ghastly developments would have developed.

Anyway, I ate my chocolate marshmallow nut sundae all unknowing. We even lingered longer than usual, because we were discussing the Heart Hop and that is a very delectable topic of conversation.

The Heart Hop is a dance which is given every year in October by one of the girls' clubs at high school. It is terribly splash and everyone gets new formals and has a super time. But the big difference between the hop and other dances is that the girls invite the boys, which, for once, gives us the privilege of picking instead of being picked. Not, of course, that I had any intention of asking anyone but Brose. In fact, all the girls seemed to take it for granted that I must have already asked him, so I didn't tell them I hadn't actually got around to doing it yet.

"Just think," Kay Lamb drooled ecstatically, "it's less than two weeks off."

Barbie Walters gloated, "I'm glad I've got a man all spoken for. Nobody's left undated now but a few ghouls."

"Me, too," Kay echoed. "I asked Itchy ages ago. Can't

be too careful about an important thing like the Hop."

Barbie nodded sagely, scraping the last smidgin of chocolate from the bottom of her dish. "We really don't appreciate how lucky we are. Why, Mary Andrews came right out and admitted to me she's almost desperate because she hasn't got a date all set yet for the Hop. And look how cute she is."

"Oh, I don't know," I said. I'd had a little trouble with Brose once over Mary and so maybe I was prejudiced.

"Anyway," Barbie said, "we're pretty lucky, having Itchy and Sox and Brose all sort of permanently attached to us. Sometimes I think a girl takes an awful chance just playing the field like Mary does. She's so likely to get stuck sometimes."

Even with all that portentous conversation on the subject, I didn't suffer a single qualm of foreboding. After all, Brose knew I'd ask him, even if I hadn't got around to it yet. Hadn't I always asked him to the Heart Hop? But little did I realize what a super sabotage job my little sister was doing to my long-standing relationship with Brose practically that very minute.

Chapter Seventeen

COMPLICATIONS

*M*idge had gone over to Judy's to play when I got home. Not that I paid any particular attention to her whereabouts. I wrote some in my diary and did my nails and decided I'd mention the Heart Hop to Brose the next day and tell him I'd like to have him go with me.

Dinner was much as usual, except that Midge seemed rather quiet, which should have aroused my suspicions, but didn't. Mom had had a letter from Janet and we were all anxious to hear the news. It seemed she was feeling fine again and could hardly wait until January.

"We're going to be grandparents with a vengeance," Dad chuckled. "Somehow I always felt sort of like an amateur with just one grandchild."

Mom said, "I hope it's a girl. A little sister for Toots would be so sweet."

"Well, yes," Dad agreed, "so long as she doesn't over-do it. We need a few boys in the family to even things up."

"Why doesn't Alicia have a baby?" Midge inquired. "She's been married five months now."

"Might make it a little crowded around their Quonset hut," Dad suggested. "Although I suppose it's only a matter of time—"

"Henry," Mom interrupted, giving him a look, "why don't you pass the salad? Someone might like some more."

"I still think it's foolish of Alicia and Adam," Midge insisted, "wasting a lot of time . . ."

It was much later, just before she was ready to start up to bed, that Midge got around to informing me, "Oh, Tobey, I nearly forgot. Brose called you this afternoon."

"Well, fine!" I exclaimed with justifiable sarcasm. "Just tell me about these things any time!"

We were alone in the hall. Mom was writing to Janet in the library and Dad was playing over his Spike Jones records. It struck me that Midge had picked this particular time to tell me about Brose's call, instead of blurting it out in front of everybody, which would have been more like her.

"What did he want," I asked, "if it isn't too much trouble?"

My sister twisted the end of one of her sandy braids around her finger. She seems to imagine this will eventually make her hair curl, although it certainly hasn't had any effect so far. "He—uh—didn't say. He—hung up sort of—sudden."

It struck me that Midge was acting very odd.

"Look," I said sternly, "let's begin at the beginning. What did he say and what did you say? And no funny business!"

Midge gulped, "Well, he called up and asked where you were. And I figured it wouldn't hurt him to get a little jealous. It's never a good idea to let a man be too sure of you, Aunt Flora says, because then they—"

"Leave Aunt Flora out of this," I cut in grimly. "What did you tell Brose?"

"Well," my sister tried to hedge, "I knew you prob'ly wouldn't want me to tell him, but I figured—"

"Not want you to tell him what?" I demanded.

"Where you'd gone," Midge said.

I guess I must have stared at her pretty blankly, because she went on, "I just told him what you said when you left, that you were going out with some boy named Taylor."

"Taylor?" I repeated stupidly.

Midge's eyes widened in genuine astonishment. "That was what you said, Tobey—wasn't it?"

Going out with someone named Taylor, going to the tailor with a coat—I suppose they do sound alike to a person intent on reading advice to the lovelorn. But I wasn't in any mood at the moment to be forebearing.

"You little dope!" I berated her. "I wasn't out with anyone! I took my coat to the tailor and that was exactly what I told you! If you'd listen . . ."

Midge sniffed ominously and I knew she was all set to start bellowing, which would probably bring Mom or Dad or both of them down on us and only complicate matters further. And, goodness knows, they were already complicated enough!

"Stop it!" I commanded in a low but stern voice. "I'll call him back and explain. But next time don't go garbling my messages."

With that I left her and went to phone Brose. Kid sisters! Why are they, I wondered, as I gave the operator Gilman's number.

Brose's mother answered. She seemed a little surprised when I asked if he was home. "Why, Tobey, didn't he go to the movies with you?"

I felt a swooping sensation in my tummy. "Why, no," I gulped.

"Well—I guess he must have gone alone then—or with one of the boys." I could tell Mrs. Gilman was just trying to be tactful. "Shall I tell him to call you when he gets home?"

"Never mind," I said, "I'll see him at school tomorrow. It can wait till then."

I thanked her and hung up. It was perfectly apparent that Brose had taken some other girl to the movies. His mother had just assumed it was I, because he usually did take me. The swooping sensation in my tummy grew worse. But before I fell asleep I had reasoned myself into a calmer frame of mind. After all, I could explain everything to him in the morning . . .

When I encountered Brose at school next day it was in the hall near the lockers. I thought for a minute he was simply going to pass me by with just a cool, "Hi, hag."

Brose is definitely inclined to be jealous, which I've always felt was sort of thrilling and flattering. But I couldn't let him get into a tailspin over absolutely nothing.

"Look, tall, handsome, and hot-headed," I teased with my very most winning smile. "Doesn't the condemned even get a chance to defend herself?"

"It's a free country," Brose said, his arms crossed and his chin sort of jutting forward. "You can go out with anyone you please, even perfect strangers named Taylor. But it works both ways."

I shook my head. "It's all just a silly misunderstanding cooked up by my poisonous little sister."

"I suppose you don't even know anybody named Taylor," Brose said nastily.

I let that ride and went on to explain exactly where I had been the previous afternoon when he phoned.

"You were—at the tailor's?" Brose repeated blankly when I had finished.

"If you doubt my word, Mr. D.A.," I kidded, "you can check my alibi with Barbie or Kay or Liz. We all had chocolate—"

"Wait!" There was a stricken look on Brose's face. One of the things I like best about the guy, he's always appalled to find himself in the wrong and he doesn't hesitate to admit it.

I stood there, smiling up at him, waiting for the apology that was sure to come. But instead of apologizing, Brose croaked in a tone of utter dismay, "But, Tobey, gee whiz, if you weren't out with some other guy . . . Well, gosh, it's this way . . . Uh—you see—I was so sore when Midge told me that, I took Mary Andrews to the movies."

"That's oke," I said magnanimously, although I wished it might have been anyone but Mary. Some people find her very attractive, but she always makes me want to arch my back and scratch. "After all," I added, "how were you to know Midge had been listening in on the wrong wave length?"

Brose was dragging at the neck of his sport shirt as though it choked him. "Tobey, gosh, this is awful! The thing is . . . Well, you see, I was so sore last night that when Mary invited me to take her to the Heart Hop— well—I figured you could just go with your new friend Taylor. So I—I said, 'yes.'"

Now I know what they mean in stories when they say people felt as though they'd been turned into ice. Brose— he couldn't do this to me! Not when I'd been counting on him, taking it for granted that we'd go to the Hop together. And now to have him take that slinky Mary Andrews, of all people! Barbie's remark of yesterday echoed ominously in my mind. "Nobody's left undated but a few ghouls!" And I hadn't even felt a qualm of premonition.

I think I smiled. At least, I felt my lips sort of part. And I managed to say quite casually, "Why, that's all right, Brose."

He stared at me. "It is?"

"Why, yes." I actually achieved an airy little laugh. Honestly, I was surprised at myself. I said lightly, "You see, I—I've been wondering how to break it to you—but I've already invited someone else to the Hop."

Thank goodness, the bell rang just then and I was able to dash for class, leaving Brose gazing blankly after me. I couldn't have kept up that ghastly pretense much longer.

The rest of the day passed in a kind of dull, aching void. I was grateful nobody, even my closest friends, knew the full extent of my predicament. I hadn't actually told anyone I was going to ask Brose to the dance. So all I had to do was think of someone else to invite—but that was the stumbling block. A quick desperate survey of the field showed me Barbie had been absolutely right. My thoughts cringed away from the sorry specimens still left undated. Okay, then I had to find a date outside of the high school crowd. But where?

My mind grew groggy in the next couple of days, going around in circles. Friends were beginning to press me as to whom I had invited to the Hop, especially since Mary Andrews hadn't wasted any time about letting everyone know she was going with Brose. I couldn't play mysterious about my plans indefinitely. Already Barbie Walters was a little hurt because we were best friends and still I wouldn't tell her whom I had invited. I was really on a spot!

And then, right in the midst of my desperation, an idea hit me. Really, it's sort of wonderful, I think, the way I get ideas just when things look blackest. Of course, they don't always work out exactly as I figure they will. But on the whole, I think probably fifty percent of my ideas have been successful. And anyone who wants a larger percentage than that simply isn't a gambler at heart.

This latest scheme of mine was really a lulu! Examine it as I would, I couldn't see a flaw in it. The whole thing was really so simple it scared me.

I didn't actually have to go to the Heart Hop with anyone! So long as I dreamed up a really impressive date to tell Barbie and Kay and the rest of my girl friends about, who would be the wiser if my dream man sprained his ankle or something on the very eve of the dance? Of course, it would be a disappointment not to get to go to the Hop. But I hadn't done anything drastic like getting a new dress for it yet. My pride would be saved, at any rate. And, after all, I wasn't in any position to quibble.

Chapter Eighteen

DREAM MAN

I figured out all the details in the privacy of my diary. This was a scheme of considerably more magnitude than I had ever undertaken before. Every angle had to be plotted in advance so I wouldn't run any risk of tripping myself up. The last thing I wanted was any slip that would put me in a ridiculous position.

My first step was to invent a boy named Jon Hayward. I have always loved the name Jon with no 'h' in it and have never met anyone whose parents were considerate enough to call him that. I picked the last name by shutting my eyes and jabbing my finger at a page in the phone book. With that settled my next step was to figure out a place for Jon to be from. This was most important. He couldn't be from Edgewood, natch, because then my friends would wonder why they had never met him. On the other hand, it wouldn't be plausible to have him from too far away, or they might wonder how I ever met him. I finally decided to have Jon live in Whitfield which is only about twenty miles from our town. Moreover, we have relatives there, so it would seem reasonable to suppose he was someone I had met when visiting Aunt Louise.

When I calmly announced one night at dinner that I was going to the Heart Hop with Jon Hayward of Whitfield, my family swallowed this myth hook, line and sinker. Their calm acceptance of my statement made me feel a little ashamed, but I kept my fingers crossed under the table all the time I was discussing Jon, so it didn't seem quite so much as though I were telling whoppers.

Dad said mildly, "If he's someone Louise knows, he must be all right."

And Mom said, "Of course, he's all right or Tobey wouldn't have invited him to the dance, would you, dear?"

I shook my head and a slight frown wrinkled Mom's forehead. "But—what about Brose? Won't he be expecting you to go with him?"

Midge said solemnly, "It's a mistake to let a man get too sure of you. Aunt Flora says so. Aunt Flora—"

"And who," my father inquired, "is Aunt Flora? I wasn't aware that either your mother or I had any sisters named Flora."

Midge fixed him with an appalled stare. "You mean you never heard of Aunt Flora?"

"She writes a revolting column in the News on love problems," I supplied. "And I'm getting pretty sick of hearing about her second-hand. Midge is forever quoting her."

Midge said, "That's a fine way for you to talk! Why, if it wasn't for me telling you how Aunt Flora says women shouldn't let men take them for granted, you'd prob'ly just be going to the Heart Hop with Brose instead of getting yourself a brand-new man with a romantic sounding name like Jon Hayward."

"Is that so?" I began hotly.

But my father interrupted, chuckling, "Now, kids, take it easy. Nothing to fight about that I can see. Tobey's got a date for the dance. Midge's confidence in Aunt Flora's advice remains unshaken." He fixed me with a thoughtful, expectant glance. "You were going to say something more about the dance, Tobey?"

I shook my head. "No, that was all I was going to say."

Dad and Mother exchanged wondering looks.

Mother repeated incredulously, "That was all?"

Dad asked, "No requests, suggestions, hints along the line of not having a thing to wear but some terrible old rag you've worn at least twice before?"

"Oh—oh, you mean about a formal." I laughed casually. "I think my yellow one will do very well for the Heart Hop. You see Jon hasn't taken me to a dance before, so any dress I wear will be new to him."

My father stared at me. "Is this my child speaking, my little Tobey, implying that she *doesn't* need a new dress?"

Mom said doubtfully, as though she couldn't quite believe the evidence of her own ears, "But that's so sensible of you, dear."

"Well—everybody has to get sensible sometime," I said, not very brightly . . .

I felt a little guilty over fooling Mom and Dad, but there simply was no other way out of the dilemma in which I found myself involved. It was the next day over malteds at Joe's Grill that I confided to Barbie that I was going to the Hop with Jon.

"So that's what all the mystery's been about," she exclaimed, her dark eyes shining excitedly behind her harlequin glasses. "An absolutely new man—one who doesn't even live here, that none of your friends have even seen. How super!"

"I'd have told you sooner," I explained, "but I had to find out for absolutely sure he could come first."

Barbie leaned her chin on her palm and stared dreamily into space. "A man named Jon—I've always wanted to meet one. Without an 'h', I mean. Aren't you just thrilled, Tobey?"

I nodded.

"No wonder you didn't care when Mary asked Brose—" she broke off to stare at me questioningly. "This doesn't mean you and Brose are all washed up, does it? You haven't gone phtt?"

"Oh, no. Brose and I are still friends—very good friends. But—" I shrugged, "I'd never want to make the mistake of letting a man feel too sure of me." I colored a little, realizing how close I had come to quoting Aunt Flora. "Besides," I hurried on, "we aren't engaged or anything really serious. There's no reason either of us isn't perfectly free to go out with someone else."

Barbie nodded thoughtfully, taking a sip of her malted. Then she asked, "what's he like—this Jon? He sounds dreamy!"

I crossed my fingers tight under the table. "Well, he's tall—and not too heavy, but his shoulders are nice and broad."

"Football?" Barbie asked interestedly.

"You know, I never asked him."

Barbie nodded. "I'll just bet he plays. Is he dark?"

"N-no, sort of blond, with nice blue eyes," I elaborated shamelessly, "and a kind of cleft in his chin."

Barbie sighed deeply. "Tell me more."

"Huh-uh," I said. "That's all I'm going to tell you. Wait till the Hop and you can see him for yourself."

"Jeepers," Barbie murmured raptly, "and I'm only going with Sox! You're lucky!"

Of course, it took practically no time for all the rest of my friends to hear about Jon. News like that travels fast. Sometimes I almost caught myself believing he was real, just as I'd convinced everyone else he was. And then I'd remember and realize this would be the first Heart Hop I'd miss since I'd been in high school. And I'd feel pretty glum.

Brose happened to catch up with me on the stairs at school during one of my low moments.

"I'd give you a penny for 'em," he cracked, "but it might help bring on inflation."

"Oh, hi, Brose," I said, unable at the moment to think of a snappy comeback.

We stood there on the stairs for a minute just looking at each other. By one of those curious twists of circumstance, there wasn't another soul in sight at the moment; we were quite alone.

Brose said, his voice a little husky, "Gee, Tobey—I hear you're going to the dance with some guy from Whitfield."

I nodded. "And you're going with Mary Andrews, remember?"

Brose said unhappily, "Gee—well, of course, I hope you'll have a swell time—I hope I will, too—" He broke off, then finished in a kind of rush, "But I sure wish we were going together."

My heart sort of jumped. But I said coolly, "Better not let Mary hear you say a thing like that."

Brose asked, "At least save me a dance, will you, Tobey?"

"If I have any to spare," I told him and went on down the stairs and left him standing there.

Honestly, life is so complicated sometimes . . .

A few days before the dance my father had to go to Cleveland on a business trip. The night before he left he and Mom came into the library where I was sort of half-heartedly doing my homework. There were wide smiles on both their faces and Dad was carrying a big flat box with Sandra's Frocks printed on the cover. I stared at it a little blankly, my heart skipping a beat, because Sandra's is my very most favorite dress shop in all Edgewood.

Mom said, beaming, "You tell her, Henry."

Dad handed me the big box, explaining, "You see, Tobey, it's this way. Your mother and I felt you were entitled to a new dress for the dance, if for no other reason than the fact you didn't press us for one. Even parents are human, baby—and your Mom remembers how she used to feel about school dances." He chuckled. "Besides, now that we've only got one daughter at home old enough to step out, we figure she ought to do the family proud."

I guess I just stood there, staring at them sort of blankly, the box in my hands.

"Well, open it, dear," Mom laughed. "See what you think of it."

My fingers fumbled at the string and finally the box was open, the tissue paper turned back. It was the most absolutely swoony formal I'd ever had in my whole life, plaid taffeta in tones of violet and gold and black, with an off-the-shoulder neckline and a skirt so wide and rustling I couldn't even believe it! Any other time I would have been so happy and thrilled over a dress like that I'd have simply popped. Now, of all the dopey things, I began to cry.

"Why, Tobey!" Mom exclaimed. "Don't you like it?"

"It's just your size," Dad said earnestly, "but it can be exchanged of you don't care for the color."

I jumped up and threw my arms around both of them, one around each. Did any girl ever have such perfectly wonderful parents—or deserve them less?

I babbled, wiping my silly tears on the front of Dad's suit, "I love the color! It's the most absolutely terrif formal I ever saw. Th-that's why I'm crying—I'm so h-happy . . ."

Well, the new dress was perfect on me. I modeled it for Mom and Dad a few minutes later and by that time I had myself under iron control. But inside I felt awful—ashamed and contrite and wicked. But there was nothing I could do but go on with the pretense I'd started about having a date with Jon Hayward. I was in far too deep now to back out. What poet was it who said, "Oh, what a tangled web we weave, when first we practice to deceive?" I was certainly caught smack in the middle of such a web right this minute. And my sensations were just like those of the poor little helpless fly, waiting for the big bad spider to come home . . .

Dad left early the next morning for Cleveland. Time simply crawled the next few days. I was so anxious to have the night of the Heart Hop come—and go!—that I could hardly stand it. I wanted to be finished with the whole dishonest business and forget I'd ever made up a guy named Jon Hayward.

I had a shampoo and hair-set and manicure at the beauty shop the day before the dance. It would have seemed queer if I'd refused when Mom suggested it. With Dad away, Mom had more time to concentrate on me and honestly, when she spoke about getting to meet Jon and the sort of evening we'd have and everything, I felt so guilty I could have died. By Saturday morning my wave had loosened up just right, so that my hair looked sort of like a golden cloud, if I do say it myself. Mom wouldn't let me help with the dishes all day, so I wouldn't spoil my manicure, and I felt like an utter heel. As soon as I was alone in the house for a single minute, I was going to pretend to get a phone call from Jon, telling me he'd sprained his ankle and couldn't take me to the dance. But it seemed as though Mom would never go out. And, after lunch, when she finally had to do her marketing for the week-end, Midge had her pal Judy over and the two of them stuck to me like a pair of burrs.

We had a female sort of meal at dinner and by seven o'clock I still hadn't had a single chance to fake the phone call that would break my imaginary date. You can picture the state of mind I was in, with Mom insisting I start getting ready, or I'd be late, and Midge hanging around trying to be helpful. She got out my best slip and stockings and laid them carefully on my bed and even offered to put bath salts in the tub and run my bath for me.

Finally I couldn't think of another excuse for delay, so in desperation I started getting ready. What else could I do but let Mom and Midge think Jon had simply stood me up?

In spite of all I'd been through, I looked pretty super by the time I was dressed. Mom and Midge superintended the job and finally they stood back and regarded me with proud satisfaction.

Mom said wistfully, "I do think he should have sent you a corsage, darling."

Midge said, "Maybe he'll bring it when he comes."

"If he doesn't," Mom frowned, "I'll feel it's inexcusably thoughtless of him."

"He's sort of the thoughtless type," I said, grasping at any straw that presented itself. "Very absent-minded."

"But that's odd," Mom said, "in a boy so young."

"Why," I went on, "Jon's even capable of forgetting we've got a date tonight. I wouldn't put it past him at all."

"Why, Tobey," Mom gasped, "he couldn't do anything so dreadful!"

"You don't know Jon," I said faintly. "He's always forgetting things—quite important things sometimes."

"But, darling," Mom insisted, "a dance is such a big date. Surely even an absent-minded boy—" She broke off to ask anxiously, "You're sure you told him just when it was going to be and everything?"

"Oh, yes," I said. "And—of course, if he should forget it, I'd never forgive him. I wouldn't make a single other date with him as long as I live—and—and you know, I've got the oddest hunch—"

Just then the doorbell chimed and Midge, who had been perched on my bed, practically tumbled off in her excitement.

"I'll go down, Tobey," she said, beaming expectantly. "It's prob'ly Jon."

I tried to say something, but my throat closed. Besides, what could I say?

Chapter Nineteen

DICK PINCH HITS FOR JON

*M*idge trotted off down stairs and Mom fluffed out the skirt of my lovely dress and smoothed my hair and made all those affectionate little gestures mothers always make at times like this. I wanted to die, because I knew darned well there was no Jon downstairs. And I hated having Mom disappointed when she was so swell.

I got all choked up and I think in another second I'd have been weeping on her shoulder and confessing all. But then I heard Midge open the front door and a man's voice say something I couldn't quite catch.

And then Midge said, in that sort of high dramatic tone she sometimes put on to impress strangers, "You must be Jon Hayward," and I wanted to die more than ever.

But a man's voice said, "Well, no, I'm not Jon, but Jon

sent me. You see, he had the bad luck to sprain his ankle this afternoon. And rather than let your sister down entirely, he asked me to substitute for him."

"For pity's sake!" Mom exclaimed in whispered astonishment.

But she wasn't half as surprised as I. Jon had sent him, but there wasn't any Jon! My head was spinning. Who was that ancient sculptor who saw his statue come to life? I must be going mad.

My face probably reflected some of the turmoil going on within me. For Mom said solicitously, "Now, darling. It's too bad Jon hurt his ankle and couldn't come. But wasn't it nice of him to send someone in his place?"

Nice wasn't the word. It was miraculous! I opened my mouth but no words came out.

"And you said he was thoughtless," Mom went on reprovingly. "Why, I think he's very considerate!"

I gulped, "I never knew him to be so considerate before. It—really isn't like him. B-but I don't even know who that is down there!"

"Well, we'll just find out," Mom said soothingly. She slipped her hand under my elbow to lend me moral support. "Come on, dear, we'll go down together."

It was like one of those ghastly nightmares where things happen that you know just can't happen—that is, it was like that until I got far enough down the stairway to see the young man Midge was talking to. Then I felt better, much better, though still confused. He was tall, with nice broad shoulders, and he had brown hair and blue eyes with a nice twinkle. Those were the first things I saw. Then I noticed that he was holding one of those cute little cellophane florist boxes and that it contained an orchid. Evidently my fairy godmother, in addition to arranging to get him for me, had also whispered into his ear that my dress was in colors that definitely called for an orchid.

Dazedly I heard him go through his explanation again. He said that his name was Dick Allen. I kept looking at him, expecting him to fade away, but he stayed perfectly solid. Mom's eyes signaled to me that she liked him. I couldn't blame her, I liked him myself. Only how could he be there?

The next few minutes were something I never want to live through again. I finally found myself, my coat slung over my shoulders, going down our front walk with this —this ectoplasm. Mom and Midge stood in the lighted doorway behind us, so that there was nothing I could do until we were safely ensconced in the car toward which my mysterious escort propelled me.

Not until the door was shut did I let my breath out. It made quite a sound, as though I'd been holding it for hours.

"Okay," I said and my voice was pretty shaky, "let me in on the secret now, so I can play games, too."

Dick Allen threw back his head and laughed. He had such a nice laugh that after a minute I found myself laughing, too. Or maybe I was having hysterics?

"I have never," Dick chuckled, "seen anything quite so blank as your face when you came downstairs and saw me. If I had been a ghost—"

"Aren't you?" I asked.

"Hum-uh," Dick denied. "But you certainly deserve an explanation. You must have thought you were dreaming."

"I still do," I told him.

"It's like this," Dick said. "Your kid sister and my kid sister are pals. Judy Allen, you know her, don't you?"

Light began to break through. I suppose his name would have struck me sooner if I hadn't been so dazed and confused by the whole unexpected turn of events.

"We haven't lived in Edgewood very long," Dick went on, "and I'm in my first year at college, so I haven't been around enough to get to meet you." There was a little note of regret in his tone, as though he really thought he'd missed something not meeting me sooner. I began to feel a faint glow.

"Well, it seems your little sister read in your diary about the jam she'd got you into with your boy friend and what you planned to do about it. So she and Judy talked it all over and decided to fix things up."

My face felt hot with embarrassment. "Oh, they did, did they!"

"Don't be mad," Dick said. "I know how kid sisters are." I realized from his tone that we had much in common. "But this is one time I'm glad they stuck their little noses into something that was none of their business. Otherwise we wouldn't be here together."

I pointed out that there were still a few connecting links missing. "How did they get you back here from college?"

"That was easy," Dick said. "Judy wrote me an urgent

letter suggesting I come home for the week-end. She also enclosed a snapshot of you that Midge had given her. So," his tone grew hopefully apologetic, "here I am. And I hope you won't hold any part of the kids' conniving against me."

I was glad it was too dark in the car for Dick to see me blushing. After all, a girl doesn't like to have a perfectly super person like him know all about the things she confides to her diary. So those little fiends had found it under my mattress anyway! But, on the other hand, if they hadn't told him, I'd have been brooding at home this minute instead of being all set to go to the Heart Hop. And Dick and I might never have met at all!

I said, sort of choky with embarrassment, "I—don't know what to say. I feel so—so silly!"

"Don't," Dick urged warmly. "Can't we just forget the whole thing and pretend there really was a guy named Jon who sprained his ankle?"

"Well—"

"Let's say he was a college friend of mine. So it was only natural he'd send me in his place."

Dick was so nice and understanding about the whole thing, my embarrassment faded away. I began to look forward to the evening ahead. Of course, I didn't know Dick well enough yet to be able to tell whether I was going to like him as well as Brose. But I knew Brose well enough to know how he'd feel when he saw me with Dick, so handsome and assured and a college man, even if he was only in his freshman year. Brose would be fit to be tied!

"Okay," I said, laughing a little, "I never was very crazy about Jon."

"Atta girl," Dick said and started the car.

In many ways, I think it was the very nicest Heart Hop I had ever attended. For one thing my appearance with Dick created quite a furor among all my friends. I had to explain over and over about Jon having sprained his ankle and Dick pinch-hitting for him. Barbie and Kay and the rest of them could hardly wait to get me alone in the powder room to exclaim over how cute Dick was and how lucky I was.

"Imagine being disappointed by a guy named Jon without an 'h' in it and then having a perfectly super person like Dick turn up in his place!" Barbie sighed wonderingly.

And Kay added, "Nothing like that ever happens to me!"

"Your dress is so super, too!" Barbie exclaimed.

"*And* your orchid," Kay touched the lavender satin bow admiringly. "Itchy always sends gardenias. And they smell so sweet they make me kind of sick at my stomach."

"Gardenias are nice, too, though," I said. "They don't make me sick a bit. Brose usually sends gardenias."

"The difference between a college man's allowance and that of a high school senior," Barbie said pityingly. "Orchids—gardenias—ah, well, that's life."

Kay said, "I don't think Brose is having a bit of fun. Every time I've seen him he looks morbid. I don't think he likes Mary Andrews nearly as well as he does you, Tobey."

I shrugged. "He came to the Hop with her."

There was a bright glint of curiosity in Barbie's eyes as she asked, "Did he accept Mary's invitation before or after you asked Jon? I've wondered about that, Tobey."

"It was practically simultaneous," I sidestepped neatly. "But, anyway, don't you think it's a mistake for people to get into too much of a rut, to go with the same person to all the dances and things?"

Kay said doubtfully, "I don't know. You have more security, at least. That is, you know you'll never get left high and dry without an invitation to things if you have someone to sort of depend on. But—maybe it isn't so exciting . . ."

We left it at that and proceeded to powder our noses and fix our mouths and go back to the dance floor. The orchestra was just beginning to play a rumba and Dick was waiting for me. He was a really terrif dancer and yet, somehow, it wasn't the same as dancing with Brose, even if Brose does occasionally step on your toe. Dick is just as good looking as Brose, too, if not more so. And his line is a lot smoother and more sophisticated, although he isn't any wolf. By all the laws of reason and logic, I should have been perfectly happy to be at the Hop with Dick, instead of Brose. But I wasn't.

Dick said, as the music stopped, "By the way, Tobey, that fellow over there with the girl in green—he introduced himself while you were out fixing your face. Wanted to exchange dances on the next. Is that okay with you?"

My heart jumped. Mary Andrews was wearing green.

202

I looked around in the direction Dick had indicated and sure enough it was Brose he was talking about. "Why— why, yes," I said. "That's okay . . ."

So the next dance Dick danced with Mary and I danced with Brose. Somehow, I felt very much at home in his arms with his chin bumping my forehead now and then. It was a nice warm feeling.

For quite awhile we didn't say anything at all. Then Brose spoke. "Tobey—?"

"Yes?"

"Tobey, I gotta talk to you. I gotta talk seriously."

"Well, go ahead."

"Not here," Brose said, "with all these millions of people around, bumping into us and hearing what we say and —and everything."

"Well, where then?"

"Outside," Brose said hopefully, his arm tightening a little around me.

But there would be people outside, too. Lots of people. There always were during dances. Besides, I had a better idea, much better. All I had to do was make Brose think he'd thought of it.

I shook my head. "Our dance is almost over. And it wouldn't be very polite to Dick—and Mary—if we went outside now and they didn't know where to find us."

"I don't care whether Mary ever finds me," Brose said morosely. "But—I suppose it's different with you and Dick."

"Dick is very sweet," I said. "Very polite and considerate. I certainly wouldn't want to do anything rude to him."

"But he isn't the guy you asked to the Hop in the first place."

"No," I admitted. And then I added, because it is so much fun to torment Brose, "Jon is very sweet, too."

"Yeah," Brose said, getting out of step and landing on my toe. "Oh, I'm sorry, Tobey. But—all these guys—guys I didn't even know you knew—" He broke off to demand unhappily, "What's happened to us—to you and me, Tobey?"

"Has anything happened?"

Brose gulped, "We haven't had a date in two weeks—not since before Mary asked me to the dance."

"You haven't asked me for a date, have you?"

"Well—everything was such a mess. It still is! But—I figured once this dumb Heart Hop was over—why—we could get things straightened out between us again."

"Is that what you wanted to talk to me about?"

"Sure, but you won't even go outside with me."

"Our dance is over now," I said as the music stopped and a smattering of applause broke out. Thank goodness, Dick and Mary were clear across the room from us. It would take several minutes for us to get together, with all that crowd between. And maybe that would be time enough for me to implant an idea in Brose's mind, make him think it was his own idea.

I said, "Well, tonight isn't the end of the world. We can talk some other time."

"Tomorrow!" Brose exclaimed, fixing me with a stern

204

look, his jaw sort of jutting forward in a way I loved. "Or do you already have a date with Dick tomorrow—or Jon?"

I shook my head. "Not yet I haven't."

"Okay!" Brose's tone was almost violent and my heart pounded, I was so thrilled.

"What time tomorrow?" I inquired.

"As early as possible," Brose said. His eyes widened at a sudden idea—maybe it was mental telepathy, or something, I'd been willing him to get the idea so hard. "Look— how about going on a bike hike with me? We could take some hot dogs along and stuff and cook our lunch. Gee— will you, Tobey? It'd be just like old times."

Mary and Dick were almost with us, I noted through the corner of my eye, as I said quickly, "Okay, Brose. Tomorrow at eleven. I'll be ready . . ."

Chapter Twenty

THE CLASS RING

O f course, it would have to rain the next morning! Honestly, on such an important day, wouldn't you think the weather could co-operate? But I put on my blue jeans and plaid flannel shirt anyway, just in case.

As I went past Midge's room on my way down to breakfast, I heard sounds of her moving around, so I went in and shut the door firmly after me. She turned from her dresser where she stood braiding her hair, and looked at me with a slightly scared expression.

"Did you—have fun, Tobey?" Her tone sounded a little scared, too.

I nodded. "But that doesn't mean it was okay for you and Judy to read my diary."

"I know," Midge said. "But—if we hadn't you wouldn't

have got to go to the Hop. And—Dick is cute, don't you think?"

"He is," I admitted, "but that still doesn't alter the—the ethics of the situation. Can't you understand that diaries are private?"

"But yours is so int'resting, Tobey," Midge said.

My mouth wouldn't stay as stern as I wanted it to. I hoped I could keep my tone forbidding and severe. "If I ever catch you reading it again, I'll skin you alive, so help me."

Midge said huffily, "Well, okay if you want to be like that. Next time you get into a jam making up imaginary dates—"

"And whose fault was it I had to make up a date?"

"Well—how was I to know Brose would do something drastic like promising to go with someone else?"

"That," I said severely, "is neither here nor there. But—uh—so long as you did what you could to help me out after you'd got me into a jam—well, if you look down in the refrigerator, there's something you can have."

"In the refrigerator?" Midge sounded mystified.

"My orchid," I told her. "It's practically as good as new."

Midge's eyes began to shine. "Gee, Tobey—that's wonderful! I never had an orchid before."

"Well, you've got one now," I said and turned on my heel to march out before things began to get sticky.

Midge called after me in a penetrating whisper, "Gee, thanks, Tobey. And your secret's absolutely safe. Judy and I made a pact we'd never tell a soul about you making Jon up—only Dick. And Judy swore him to absolute secrecy, too."

"Okay," I said, "okay. Let's forget it now . . ."

Over breakfast, natch, Mom and Midge had to hear all the details about the Heart Hop and whether I'd had fun and how I liked Dick. I didn't mind telling them about everything. Midge's eyes had a sort of expectant gleam while I talked and I knew she was looking forward in her thoughts to the time when she'd be old enough to go to the Hop and get a formal and everything. I glanced at Mom and her face had a pleasant, reminiscent smile on it, so I suppose she was looking back fondly on the time when she'd done all those things, too. I felt sort of warm inside despite my disappointment over the weather, and almost happy. Telling Mom and Midge about the dance and see-ing the way they enjoyed it vicariously gave me a nice sensation as though we were all sort of knitted together in a kind of kinship, just being women, even if we hadn't been related in any other way.

And then, all of a sudden Midge exclaimed, "Look—the sun's out!"

And sure enough it was. So that made everything quite perfect, because it was still only a quarter till eleven, so Brose and I could have our bike hike and our serious talk after all!

My face must have brightened considerably, because Mom said, laughing a little, "Well, darling! Don't tell me a little rain depresses you that much. After all, you have

208

to expect it this time of year."

"I know," I said, "but not today. You see I've got a date to go on a sort of picnic."

"With Dick?" Midge asked excitedly.

"Oh, no. With Brose."

"But Dick's so much cuter," Midge argued. "And besides I thought you weren't going to let Brose—"

"If you quote Aunt Flora to me just once more," I warned her, "I'll sock you!"

And Mom put in, laughing a little, "Oh, I don't know that Dick's cuter. They're both attractive. Besides, it's Tobey's own business."

I jumped up and went around the table and hugged her. She really is swell. And then, rather to my own surprise, I gave Midge a hug, too, even after all the trouble she'd been to me. I just seemed to love everybody that morning.

Brose and I got under way a little while later. We had stowed hot dogs and buns and potato chips and cokes and cookies in our bike baskets. Brose was wearing blue jeans and a plaid flannel shirt, too, and the sun felt warm across our shoulders and there was a nice fresh smell all around.

"It's as though it rained just especially to wash the world up all nice and clean for us," I said, sniffing enjoyably.

And Brose grinned, "Yeah. But that's not the way I felt about it half an hour ago. Was I mad when I got up and saw it was raining!"

"So was I."

Brose said, "Gosh, Tobey—" his voice sort of choked and he didn't go on.

But I knew what he meant. I felt the same way.

We pedaled out past Lake Ellen and took the graveled road. I remembered so well from last winter. On New Years it had been all hard packed and crunchy with snow. Now there were fields covered with corn stubble on either side and here and there a farmhouse, with a big red barn behind and cows and pigs and an occasional horse browsing around. It had grown warmer and the sky was as blue as I had ever seen it, with scarcely a cloud. So the weather had decided to co-operate, after all.

Suddenly Brose exclaimed, "Look, Tobey—right over there. Remember that fence?"

I remembered it. Only a little of it had stuck up above the snowbank before. Of one accord we stopped our bikes and without another word being said we leaned them over at the edge of the ditch and went across and perched on the old weather-blackened top rail of the fence.

I asked, as my shoulder settled comfortably against Brose's, "Is this where you were headed all the time?"

He nodded. "It's a good place for a talk. Don't you think so, Tobey?"

"We had a good talk here New Years," I admitted.

Brose said, "I think we ought to have another one. Everything's been so—so mixed up lately, Tobey. I hate things all mixed up between us. I want them all nice and clear."

I said, "But it hasn't been my fault."

"Well—I guess it's been mostly mine."

"First Kentucky Jackson came between us."

"Let's not go that far back," Brose gulped. "Besides, she didn't really come between us. She was just a sort of—well, a mistake on my part."

"I forgave you for Kentucky," I admitted. "But then there was Mary Andrews."

"I don't care a hoot for Mary Andrews and you know it," Brose said. "I only said I'd take her to the Heart Hop because Midge told me you were out with someone else."

"And that wasn't even so," I said perversely.

"But you had asked someone else to the Hop," Brose accused. "Some drip you never even told me you knew!"

"Jon's no drip," I contented myself with saying. I wasn't going into all that at the moment, although I might tell Brose the whole truth sometime. "Besides, if you only brought me out here to blame me for everything—"

Brose's fingers closed around mine. "I didn't, Tobey. I'm not blaming you. It's just—well, gosh, I still like you better than any other girl. But I don't know how you feel about me anymore. I don't know at all!"

He sounded so utterly miserable, I was thrilled. Besides, my heart felt all fluttery with him holding my hand so hard.

I said, "But I still like you, Brose. I still like you a lot."

"More than any other boy?" Brose asked. "The way you did New Years?"

I thought about it for a long minute, but it wasn't really necessary. I nodded. "More than any other boy I've met so far."

"But, gee!" Brose gasped, fumbling with his free hand in

the pocket of his flannel shirt. "Gee, that's wonderful, Tobey. Then maybe you'll still wear this like you said you might."

He brought out something that glittered in the bright sunshine and held it out toward me in the palm of his hand.

"Your class-ring," I breathed. "Oh, Brose, I didn't realize you'd got it. It's beautiful."

I took it in my fingers and studied it, the gold circle with the Edgewood High School crest, the year of Brose's graduation.

He said, "I haven't even worn it yet. I was—saving it for you, Tobey, hoping you hadn't changed your mind."

"I haven't changed my mind, Brose," I said in a little breathless rush. "So long as it just means what we said, that we're best friends, that we like each other more than anyone we've met so far, that we hope that's the way it'll always be, but if it isn't—"

"Don't say any more," Brose stopped me. "That's what it means, Tobey. Can I put it on you?"

"Wait." I reached up and took a ribbon out of my hair, wrapped it around the inside of the ring. "I'll fix it with some thread or tape or something later, but this'll do for now."

When I'd finished I put out my right hand and Brose slipped the class-ring on my finger. Then he did a very sweet thing. He lifted my hand to his face and laid his cheek against it for a minute and then he kissed my hand. No man had ever kissed my hand before in my whole entire life! I felt all warm and soft and quivery inside and so

happy I could scarcely breathe. It made me forget Dick
and even Mary Andrews and Kentucky Jackson. At that
moment it seemed as though Brose and I were the only two
people in the world—and I liked feeling that way. I liked
it very much indeed!

Apparently Brose was experiencing similar emotions.
All he could say was, "Gee, Tobey—gee . . ."

We sat there on the old farm fence smiling at each other,
with the sun pouring down over us and the sky so blue
and everything smelling so wonderful and fresh. I wondered if there would ever be another day quite like this, so
perfect in every detail, something to treasure and look
back on.

4759